Two Minut

G000166564

Hans Seesarun was born c
Bornes Hospital in Maurit.___ ____ _____
when he was 8 and his father Ram worked at the District
Council in Mauritius and later as an Operations Director
for the NHS in London. His mother Lila worked as a Lab
Technician at Moorfield Eye Hospital. The young Hans
grew up surrounded by books. 'I love books,' he has said.
Hans wanted to be a writer from an early age. He left home
at 18 for Bangor University in Wales to study business.
Two minutes past midnight is his first thriller. He
conceived the idea in January 2017 on new year's day. He
scribbled notes on anything he could find and built up a
mass of notes, many of which were scribbled on odd bits of
paper.

am / pm

Two Minutes Past Midnight

Hans Seesarun

Boathouse Publishing

BOATHOUSE PUBLISHING
London
www.boathousepublishing.com

Boathouse Publishing

ISBN-13: 978-2990492171

ISBN-10: 2990492178

DEDICATION

This book is dedicated to the victims of PTSD. 10% of all royalties from this book will be donated to Assist Trauma Care. Assist Trauma Care employs experienced therapists trained to work with Post-Traumatic Stress Disorder (PTSD) and the after-effects of trauma in line with current evidence-based practices.

Doctor Addison

Monday, 2nd February 2015

Morning

'I came to you because I wanted to tell my story,' said the man on my couch.

His name was Amar. Flicking through the notes gathered together by my nurse Sophie, I read that he lived in south London and worked in advertising. A scribbled addendum in Sophie's blotched handwriting stated that his grandmother had just passed away.

'I don't know what to do,' he said. 'I have prayed, but I am not religious. So I came here instead.'
Amar lay straight as a yardstick on the couch. His feet protruded stiffly over the end. His arms rigid at his side and his face was carefully set.

'My parents and my two sisters were all murdered that night and I just cowered in a closet and did nothing. I just want to tell you everything that I know,' said Amar.

'Okay, I'm listening,' I said, 'but I thought that your family were all killed in a car accident?'

'That's what I've been telling myself but it's not the truth. I have disguised the truth for all these years and I am sick of it. It's what my grandmother would tell me to say to the other kids at school,' explained Amar.

I started looking through my notes to see if there was any information on this but there wasn't.

'It happened on Tuesday the 5th 1993 and back then I thought that I was too young to understand anything and so I just let the grown-ups handle everything. But looking back, I should have done more. My birthday is on the 1st of January. The first week of the first month of the year. Something to commemorate. My parents named me Amar which in Hindi means undying, deathless, fadeless, and perdurable. My father worked in large brokerage firm and my mother was a typical housewife. We lived in a small quiet town called Montagne Blanche.'

I waited, saying nothing. Amar looked haggard and old. His hair was thinning and his complexion was sallow. His eyes held all the miserable secrets of alcohol and amphetamines.

'They were all murdered, throats slit, stabbed in the stomach, back, neck and eyes.'

Amar stood up.

'What's that?' he barked. His eyes had narrowed to black slots.

'What's what?'

'That door,' he pointed.

'The closet,' I corrected him. 'Where I hang my coat and leave my shoes.'

'Do you mind if we open it?' he said.

I got up wordlessly and opened the closet. Inside, a raincoat hung on one of the hangers. I had several boxes and a pair of women's shoes. The Metro newspaper had been carefully tucked into one of them.

I said nothing and wondered why Amar had been so fascinated with my closet.

Amar turned around and returned to his previous position.

'You were saying,' I said as I went back to my chair, 'that if a suspect could be found, then all your troubles would be over.'

He abruptly replied; 'I don't think I said that but you are right, I'd know the truth.' He smiled at nothing.

'How did it happen?' I asked.

Amar twitched around and stared at me.

'I'll tell you, don't worry.'

I started making notes about Amar who looked high as a kite. He was clearly on something but I couldn't quite put my finger on it. My guess was maybe amphetamines or ketamine. His behavior was highly erratic and his speech was slurred. I spotted it straight away and noticed how sometimes his head would shake involuntarily without him realising. The longer you are in this profession, the easier it gets to identify the patient's vice.

'I was only five when it happened,' Amar said again. 'Back then, I was living with my parents in a small town called Montagne Blanche in Mauritius. The year was 1993 and I was living with my mother, father and two sisters. It was very late at night. I looked up at the clock and it read two minutes past midnight. I can remember waking up to the sound of the rain falling on a tin roof. It was loud and sounded like tiny pebbles clattering on top of a single note on a xylophone. I couldn't sleep and needed to use the toilet. I heard a scream coming from the corridor and can remember how the door to my room was slightly ajar. I lifted my head and heard more noises. I climbed out of my bed and turned on the lamp. My sisters Teha and Neha were fast asleep in their beds.'

'How old were your sisters?' I asked.

'Neha was eight and Teha was six,' he replied.

Amar closed his eyes and spoke, 'I heard more noises and so I walked out into the corridor and I can remember following a trail of blood. I followed it into the living room and found my father with his throat slit and blood pouring out of him. I screamed and ran straight to my mother's bedroom and found her bleeding profusely. She had been stabbed several times in her back and neck. I scanned the room but there was nobody there.'

Amar opened his eyes and drank from his water bottle. I was stunned; Amar's story had unsettled me.

'What happened next?' I asked. I raised my head eagerly and waited.

Amar looked unsteady. He closed his eyes, took a deep breath and spoke. 'I ran to my sister's room and found Neha and Teha with their throats slit. Everyone was dead. I was alone.'

I leaned forward and asked, 'so what happened next?'

'I was scared and I did not know what to do. I immediately hid. Whenever I played hide and seek with my sisters, I would usually hide out in this closet which looked very similar to that one over there,' pointed Amar. 'I wished that I went out and looked for a clue or something, but I was too scared. I wished that I did more,' he said.

'There was nothing that you could have done,' I said and asked him what he did next.

'I just waited,' said Amar. 'The wind was howling and the rain had stopped. I could not see out of the dark closet and so I laid perfectly quiet and still. I wish that I had heard someone - anyone but the house was quiet. I thought that maybe the killer was outside of the house and was waiting for me.'

'Are you certain that you did not hear or see anything?' I asked.

'I wish that I heard the murderer climbing out of our house through a window or a door but I heard absolutely nothing,' said Amar. 'For a second, I thought I heard footsteps in the corridor but that was probably just my mind playing tricks on me.'

'Did the police find any fingerprints, clues or forcible entry into the house?' I asked.

'I don't know Doctor Addison. Sometimes I dream that I killed my family,' he said.

'You were just a child,' I said.

'Maybe I have a split personality,' suggested Amar. 'I wished that I had seen or heard somebody else in the house. Then I would be certain that it was not me.'

He opened his eyes and it looked as though he was struggling to breathe.

'Would you like to take a break?' I suggested.

'No, it's fine,' said Amar.

'Are you sure?'

With labored breathing he continued. 'I hid in the closet and I didn't cry in case the killer overheard me. It was very hard to keep quiet and I really needed to pee,' explained Amar.

'How long were you hiding in the closet for?' I asked.

'I'm not sure but it seemed like an eternity. I decided to make a run for it. I closed my eyes and sprinted out of the corridor, tripping over one of my sister's toys. It was a porcelain doll. I landed shoulder first on to the floor and rolled to my side. Without thinking, I got up and ran straight out of the front door and into the darkness. There was no light anywhere and I could not see anything. For a moment, I thought that somebody was right behind me and I felt a grip on my shoulder. I just ran until I reached our neighbour's house. I pounded on the front door and screamed for help. I explained everything and waited for them to phone the police. The police arrived and interrogated me. They went without me to investigate the crime scene. A policeman said that it was not safe for me to stay here and he wanted to drive me to the hospital. I asked why and he replied that my shoulder had popped out of its socket. I had not even noticed. I got into the back seat, crouched down and closed my eyes. I thought that I was dreaming. I wanted to wake up from the nightmare. I thought that I would wake up any minute. I closed my eyes and woke up at the hospital. My grandmother was by my side. She was crying. After the 5th May 1993, we never went back to Montagne Blanche. I lived with my grandmother at her house in the north of the island.'

'What happened after?' I asked.

'The case has remained unsolved to this day,' pointed out Amar.

'How did you end up in Britain?' I asked.

'My grandmother decided to take me to London with her to start a new life,' he explained.

Our session had gone over the allocated time but I couldn't stop him now.

'Who do you think could have done this?' I asked.

'The thing is, I don't really know much about what happened. Deep down, I always suspected that my father had something to do with it,' said Amar.

'You think he was involved?' I enquired.

'He must have had enemies. The other night, I dreamt that the police had called me to say that they had caught the killer. But I guess I am still waiting for that day to come. I should have gone and looked for the killer years ago,' said Amar.

'It's not your job to find the killer. Leave that to the authorities,' I said.

'There are so many unanswered questions. There were no suspects and the case has never been solved,' explained Amar.

'Have you sought an assessment or help since your trauma?' I asked.

'No,' he replied.

'Why did you not open up to anyone?' I asked and thought that Amar was taught a stoical acceptance of suffering.

'Because when I think about it, it really hurts. It still hurts as much as it did back when I was only five. Maybe even more so,' he explained. He took a deep breath.

'Everytime I close my eyes, it brings back painful memories of the night of the 5th. I wished that I was older. My memory from when I was 5 is not clear and I have forgotten a lot of things. I thought that I put it all behind me. I was fine until my grandmother passed away. A year ago, things were great, I had moved to south London with my girlfriend. We bought a flat and got a cat. Everything was fine until January this year.'

'What happened?' I asked.

'We went to Italy for her birthday and we got into a huge argument. The argument was that bad that we both decided to break up for good. It hasn't been an easy year for me and just last week my grandmother passed away,' said Amar.

'I'm am sorry for your loss,' I said. 'Before I end our session I must ask, what is it that you want from therapy?'

'I just want answers,' said Amar reluctantly. 'But maybe I'm not ready. Lately, I feel as though I have nothing to look forward to.'

'Are you having appetite changes, fatigue, irritability, problems with memory, problems with concentration and feeling like you have diminished ability to feel joy and pleasure?' I asked.

'Yes,' replied Amar. 'I feel all those things.'

'The symptoms you name could reflect PTSD,' I explained. 'Have you sought any other assessment or help since your trauma? Are these symptoms taking a toll on you and your functioning?'

'This is the first time I have ever spoken to a Doctor

about my trauma,' replied Amar. 'A week ago when my grandmother passed away is when I felt like the pain had become insurmountable. Everything that I had pushed down had resurfaced.'

'I am so sorry to hear that you lost your grandmother. These are symptoms of depression which can sometimes come on as a result of grief. I really think that therapy can help you. I am going to prescribe some medication for you,' I suggested.

'What medication?' he asked indignantly.

'SSRI,' I said. 'Antidepressants.'

'The thing is,' Amar paused, 'I really hate the idea of prescription drugs. I don't trust them. Can I have some time to think about it?'

'Of course,' I replied. 'Is there anything that you want to tell me before we end our first session?'

'I can't think of anything,' replied Amar who stopped and had a long and hard thought.

'My drinking has gotten really bad but that started when my ex and I broke up in January,' said Amar reluctantly.

'Thank you for admitting that,' I said. 'Amar I want you to feel comfortable here. Everything that we discuss here, stays here. Sometimes people drink excessively to cope. I am not here to pass judgment, I am here to help you.'

Amar smiled.

I was glad that Amar had come clean about his drinking and I was sure that he would tell me about the drugs when he felt that he trusted me.

'When is our next session?' he asked.

'On Thursday,' I replied and smiled.

'Thank you Doctor Addison,' he said.

Amar shook my hand and left.

Amar

Monday 2nd February 2015

Afternoon

I left Doctor Addison's office and went straight to the toilet. I latched the cubicle door and emptied out my wallet. There were a few plastic containers. Some with ketamine, one had amphetamines and the other had coke. I had mixed up the bags.

Maybe I wanted somebody to catch me that day. I should have come clean to Doctor Addison but I did not want her to judge me. I remembered her saying that her job was to not judge and that it was to help.

I thought about her long hair and tanned skin. She had probably just come back from a trip to the Bahamas. If I took her in my arms, she would smell of berries and powdered sugar.

This was a stupid idea. I came here for medical help but all I could think about was Doctor Addison and how drop dead gorgeous she was. It was fine because she was very attractive in an obvious kind of way, so it was okay to think about her like that. I think that if I did not see her like that, then there would definitely be something wrong with me.

I should have come clean about the drugs but I only took them occasionally. I wasn't at risk. I wasn't high all the time. When my grandmother passed away the pain was unbearable. I was all alone and I had no one to confide in. The ketamine numbed my body and helped me to forget. I should have mentioned it to the Doctor but I believed that it was helping me to cope. The last thing I needed now were prescription drugs, which can be a million times more addictive.

Maybe therapy was a bad idea. This was what I was afraid of. First, it's the medication and then after that they will stick me in a straight jacket in a padded room.

I steadied my hand and used my house key to scoop up some of the powder, carefully balancing it. Once it was still, I took a snort and instantly felt the taste in the back of my throat. It tasted like speed. Just what I needed. I had forgotten my water bottle in Doctor Addison's office. I was going to grab one from the shop before I got on the train. I closed my eyes and felt relaxed and thought about floating but speed doesn't make you feel like that.

I wished that I had not mixed up the bags. What I really needed right now was some Ketamine. I'll have to wait until I get home.

I patted my trouser to dust off any remaining traces of white powder that had fallen out of the bag. I flushed the toilet even though I didn't use it. I stood opposite the mirror to stare at my reflection. I looked old and haggard.

When I looked in the mirror I could barely recognize myself. It wasn't me. At least, not the me I knew.

I splashed some water on my face and on my way out, the nurse said goodbye to me. I caught everyone's head discreetly turning towards me. It was subtle, but the signs were too familiar. They were probably all judging me, whispering between themselves as soon as I'd left the room, talking about the addict in the bathroom. I sniffed and quickly wiped my nose.

I took the elevator down and walked to Waterloo station, boarding the first train to Surbiton. The departures board flashed as I ran across the concourse: delays again.

Probably another person jumping on the tracks. It was a favourite spot for the suicidals. I thought about suicide quite often when I boarded the Southwestern train. But to actually jump in front of a train? It was so final. I could never do it. But I believed that everyone has thought about suicide at one point in their life.

Once I dreamt that I was swimming in a beautiful coral reef, with tropical fish slipping in between the undercurrents and I unhooked my scuba gear. It actually felt like I was slowly slipping away until I woke up from the dream and I was out of breath. The dream felt real and I felt like I was drowning.

James Kirkup once wrote that, "the sad thing is that suicide doesn't end the pain. It just passes it onto someone else."

I agree but what if you have no one to pass this pain over to? I really miss my grandmother. She was the only family I had left in this world and now she was gone. If I died tomorrow, who would actually show up at my funeral apart from a few friends? Looking back on my life, I wished that I had invested more of my time at trying to start a family, as opposed to maintaining friendships. That's my one real regret.

Eventually the train arrived and as I slunk into my seat, I started missing my grandmother and I remembered how I had no-one. My grandmother was not the only one to leave me. My girlfriend had left me too. We were together for over five years and I never once told her about the night of the 5th. What if she thought that I was behind all the murders? I could never have taken that risk.

This year has been tough but I thought about how I could get things back to a year ago. I was actually happy and content living with my girlfriend and our cat. I used to call my grandmother every evening to tell her how my day went. So much had changed. In life you have periods of bliss and then after comes the storm. I was waiting for the storm to pass.

I thought about moving to Paris or Germany. Get a fresh start, like when I left Mauritius with my grandmother. I can't keep running away from my problems and responsibilities.

I started listening to the rhythm of the wheel on the tracks. I saw the reflection of my sallow skin in the train window.

I started picking at the plaster on my forefingers. Bruises from bumping into things while drunk. I had a feeling that I was going to feel terrible all day as soon as I got on the train and so I decided to get high.

I haven't slept properly in days. I hated this, the weight loss and insomnia. The last time I looked in the mirror I noticed how I had become extremely thin. I had been binging on takeaway food for the last few months. Sometimes when I'm crashing down, I can go for almost two days without a proper meal.

Immediately after the break up, I had been pushing myself at the gym twice a day. But during the last few months I had really let go of myself. Fuck it, I thought. What's the point? Why should I prolong the inevitable decay of my body?

God, what happened to me. I really hate the fact that I am facing this alone. I wished that I had somebody that I could confide in. Fuck it! I thought. You are born alone and you are going to die alone. I hate to think what people might think if they knew my story. They would probably judge me because I never went back to look for the killer.

As each day passed, I thought about it less and less. I wanted to find the killer but I was too much of a coward. No matter what I do, my family is not going to come back alive. They are gone. Maybe one day, the universe will fix everything, at least I hope. I don't believe in God. How can a God exist in a world like this.

I looked outside and the train was pulling into Walton on Thames. I had missed my stop. I got off and ran back to the opposite platform. It was a cold February day. The sky was grey and I thought about how it could rain at any moment. I was wearing a black trench coat and a grey sweater. I wished that I had put on a thicker coat. I was sitting at the platform, waiting for the rain to fall on me. The sky was cloudy with swallows looping and diving in the air.

I thought about my family. I wished that I had grown old together with my sisters by my side. I was only five and I don't know if we were ever truly happy. How can you miss something that you only had for a fleeting moment? Sometimes when I close my eyes, I try and picture my mother's face but I can't even remember what she looked like.

I remember playing hide and seek with my sisters and how we use to ride our bicycles. I can remember playing with fireworks on New Year's Eve and on Diwali.

It suddenly hit me. I should mention the dogs to the Doctor. How could I have forgotten that? How did that slip my mind? I guess the point of therapy was to help me remember.

My grandmother always told me that my mother and father loved me and my sisters very much and that they only wanted the best for us. I didn't get a lot of time with them.

I sometimes wonder if my grandmother ever thought that I had something to do with it all. What if I killed them in my sleep? What if I have a split personality?

I thought about Doctor Addison as I passed the pub by Surbiton station. My ex and I used to go there all the time to get breakfast in the morning or a beer after work. On the opposite side of the street was a bicycle shop. I used to ride my bicycle all the way to Richmond park. I was too lazy to walk and so I got on the K2 bus to Berrylands road.

I closed the door to my flat and I suddenly felt overwhelmingly alone again. I stared out of my window. I lit a cigarette and looked across at my neighbour's house.

The old man was watching television again. He could be dead and no one would ever know. He lived alone. Something drew me to him, I couldn't be certain what.

I used to be perfectly contented when my ex lived here with me. I miss her everyday. I still don't understand why she took the cat with her. I really miss our cat. Her name was Norah. We named her after the singer Norah Jones.

I like going to see a therapist. It feels like confession without the judgment. I just wished that Doctor Addison didn't remind me of my ex. It was her voice, soft and warm. I looked around my flat and I noticed how empty it was. I can't even pick up the telephone and call my grandma.

I sat on the couch and decided to take some ketamine. I took a snort and my head felt like it was floating. I felt like my whole body was slowly wrapping itself into a cocoon. Imagine that you are seated on a couch and it's the most comfortable place on earth. I drifted away and then I was gone.

I opened my eyes and the feeling had passed. I poured some tap water into a glass and then I went out for another cigarette.

My friend Rob once told me that my head would sometimes shake involuntarily without me even realising it. That was the ketamine. It happened the first time I took it. I am never sure whether I am doing it.

The thing about Ket is that it doesn't last very long. I hate that my mind drifts and I start thinking about my family. That's why I must take it. It helps me not to think.

I am one of those people who never trust anyone. Doctor Addison was a complete professional but I decided to get a second opinion on everything. I got in touch with a psychiatrist online. He gave me his phone number. It wasn't cheap. He was an expert. I asked him if it was okay for a Doctor to prescribe SSRI to a patient after their first session?'

He said that, 'I do think that if a Doctor has spent 2 hours hearing about your symptoms, then there is a very good chance that they have gained enough information to decide if medication could help. There are core symptoms that medications tend to help with if identified. It is often ideal to start treatment with medications sooner rather than later due to the fact they take 6-8 weeks to become effective.'

'That makes sense but I have a deep underlying fear of pills and medication,' I said.

'Evidenced-based treatment for PTSD recommends a combination of medication and therapy. Hopefully the Doctor is also working with you from a psychotherapy angle or has recommended someone in addition to him or her. Most psychiatrists manage medications more often than they provide therapy so it is possible they could be overzealous with a medication suggestion. The good news about SSRI is that they are pretty low risk to try and take. With that being said, many people can get enough support through talk therapy to overcome PTSD and depression. So if your preference is to delay treatment with medications then I think that this is completely respectable and it could make good sense to try concrete therapy for a couple months before deciding if medications are still warranted. Many people feel that they can conquer their wellbeing through non-medication approaches and it is always worth a try! Sometimes this is true and sometimes meds really can make a big difference in helping someone feel better. For now, full steam therapy is still a great option,' explained the Doctor over the telephone.

'Thank you,' I said.

His internet profile stated that his name is Doctor Max Weinberg. This was a great idea. I thought about how I could bounce back different information to always have a second opinion. I decided not to tell Doctor Addison about Doctor Weinberg. That way I can stay one step ahead of her. I really distrusted psychiatrists.

I had this recurring nightmare where I woke up in a mental institution and they were using humans as guinea pigs. They were performing a transorbital lobotomy on the other patients and I was next. First they zapped you with electro shock and then they enter slowly through your eyes with an icepick without anesthesia. They poke around in there and take a few nerve fibres out of your brain. The Nuremberg code prohibits experimenting on humans but some Doctors at these clinics have found a way around it.

That dream had always scared me. I needed to make sure that I don't get hooked on any meds and I needed to be ready to walk away from therapy if I suspect that Doctor Addison might be trying to stick me in a mental institution. I don't want to end up in a padded room. I had been fine all these years without any therapy. I bet I can get over this all by myself. I am only going there because I am yearning for change, for answers. I guess deep down I want to know the truth before it's too late. My grandmother died not knowing why her son and family were killed. I wanted to do something before it was too late.

Doctor Addison

Thursday 4th February 2015

Morning

I ran late to work this morning. I missed my connecting train at Wimbledon station. I had an appointment with a patient at 10am before Amar but I'm going to have to move things around now. My 10am thinks that he is Woody Allen. He even calls me his analyst. He has seen too many films and I get the feeling that he is trying to live out some weird fantasy. I actually can't stand him.

I am going to move him to the evening. I'm sure that he won't mind. He probably just wants to talk about how he cheats on his wife and feels guilty about it when in reality he was just coming here to brag about his infidelities. Amar is a troubled soul and needs my help. This is a great opportunity for me. Amar has an exciting story which I can maybe write about. It's the perfect murder mystery.

I wrote a children's book a few years ago. It didn't do as well as I'd hope. A career as a Doctor is great and the money is good but this was not how I thought that my life would turn out. I dreamt of really leaving a mark. It's like that book Great Expectations by Dickens. I expected a lot more out of life. I'm 35 with no children and I have never been married.

I can use Amar's story as research or I can write a non-fiction book about it. When he walked into my office, I had a feeling that I had landed on something big. An opportunity like this comes along only once in a lifetime. I needed to make him relax more around me and maybe even trust me.

With my earlier appointment moved to later on in the day, I had more time to focus on Amar. Our last session ran well over 45 minutes but this was not important. I am not going to bill him in case I scare him away.

Our session began. Amar was 10 minutes late because of signal failure on the southwestern train to Waterloo. He took a seat on my couch and crossed his fingers together.

'Before we proceed. I have to come clean about something,' he said.

'What is it?' I asked.

'I was not totally honest with you last time. The thing is that I think that I might have a drug problem.'

'What kind of drugs?' I asked him.

'Anything that I can find but mostly ket, speed and sometimes a little coke,' he said. 'I think that I have it under control. I can stop anytime but right now I don't want to stop. Well, at least not right away. I don't see what the difference is between your drugs and my drugs. Take anti-depressants.'

'What about anti-depressants?' I asked.

'I read somewhere that antidepressants reduce depression, which is a major cause of suicide,' explained Amar.

'Where did you read that?' I asked.

'On the internet somewhere. Is it true?' he asked.

'Antidepressants can trigger suicidal thoughts and suicide itself but it is also important to note that there is not consistent evidence that antidepressants increase suicide at all for adults older than 25. In fact, one study found that depressed adults, especially those older than 65, who took antidepressants called serotonin reuptake inhibitors - drugs like Prozac and Paxil - were less likely to die by suicide than those who did not take antidepressants,' I recited my university knowledge.

'Before we proceed any further, I want to make it perfectly clear that I don't want to take any medication,' said Amar. 'I'm just scared of what it might lead to.'

'What is that?' I asked.

'I don't want to end up in a straight-jacket in a padded room,' he said. 'That's the main reason why I have stayed away from therapy my whole life.'

'I am not here to put you in a mental institution. I am here to help you,' I said. 'I am very pleased that you have come clean about the drugs.'

Amar thanked me and said that he wanted to confess about everything.

'Sometimes when I am upset I get drunk and gamble but I think that I have it all under control. I am not in any danger or debt,' explained Amar.

'Everyone is different in how they cope with their problems,' I said. 'I am not here to force you to take anything that you don't want to but I think that you should immediately stop taking any drugs that has not been prescribed by a licensed medical practitioner.'

'I read an article from the BBC stating that Ketamine has 'fast-acting benefits' for depression,' Amar said. 'Is it true?'

'Ketamine has "shown promise" in the rapid treatment of major depression and suicidal thoughts,' I said. 'A recent study found that ketamine has a reputation as a party drug but is licensed as an anaesthetic. The study found use of the drug via a nasal spray led to "significant" improvements in depressive symptoms in the first 24 hours. The Royal College of Psychiatrists said it was a "significant" study that brought the drug "a step closer to being prescribed on the NHS. Antidepressants is not for everyone. I am going to recommend that you try and get some exercise. I am one hundred percent certain that this can help you.'

'I haven't gone to the gym in months. Maybe I'll go tonight,' suggested Amar.

'Maybe you can try cycling,' I said.

'I can ride my bike at Richmond park. I'll try and get some exercise tonight.'

'I think that we should try cognitive behavioral therapy.'

'What's that?' asked Amar.

'It's a type of counselling,' I said. 'It can be used to develop practical ways of dealing with your phobia. One part of the CBT treatment process that's often used to treat simple phobias involves gradual exposure to your fears, so you feel less anxious about it.'

'Does this involve any medication?' he asked.

'No,' I said. 'I'll give you an example. Let's say you have a fear of spiders. At first, we can just talk about spiders. Then I can show you pictures of spiders and gradually we can go to a Zoo and we can look at spiders from behind the glass. Then when I think that you are ready. I will get you to hold on to a spider. What do you think?'

'I like the idea,' he said.

'How is work?' I asked.

'Work is good,' replied Amar. 'My boss gave me a few months off when I explained that my grandma passed away.'

'How are your friends?' I asked.

'My friends are still around. A lot of them have gotten married or moved out of London but I still see them from time to time,' explained Amar. 'I have decided that I am going to stay away from everyone.'

'Why is that?' I asked.

'I am going through some pretty heavy stuff,' said Amar. 'I'm trying to figure out why some things seem to be harder for me than they are for other people. So I figured I could either spend the next 10 years in therapy or just spend the next month and really deal with it intensely right now. It's just more efficient. I am more comfortable with fixing this alone. I have always kept to myself. It's just easier. I guess I have a problem trusting others.'

'I think that you should reach out to someone. Maybe a family member or a friend. Do any of your friends know that your grandmother has passed away?' I asked.

'I told my friend Ray,' he said.

'I think that you should tell the rest of your friends,' I suggested.

'I'll think about it,' said Amar.

'I hate that you are facing this alone,' I said. 'You should try and open up. What's the worst that can happen?'

'You are right,' said Amar. 'It's not healthy to keep all of this bottled up.'

'I am glad that you agree,' I said. 'I'll see you next monday.'

'Actually, I was wondering?' asked Amar. 'If it's possible to move our following session to later on in the day. I really hate getting on the train during rush hour.'

'I'll speak to my receptionist Sophie to see what we can do but I think that it should be fine.' I said.

'Can we make it two hours later than our usual session?'

'Okay Amar. Goodbye and take care,' I said.

'Thank you, Doctor,' he said. 'I will see you in a few days time.'

Amar left.

Amar

Thursday 4th February 2015

Afternoon

I left the Doctor's office feeling revitalised. It felt as though a great weight had been lifted from my shoulders and my head felt clear. I had no idea that therapy was this amazing. Doctor Addison was a great psychiatrist. I should have done this years ago.

I boarded the train at Waterloo station and forgot to have a cigarette at Embankment bridge. I took a deep breath and decided that I was going to have a productive evening. No cigarettes, no drugs, no alcohol and no gambling.

I longed for days like this. I had not felt this good in ages. I am a man of self-reinvention. It's chilly outside right now, but it's beautiful. I've been up for hours. I want to run away. The train accelerated out of the station, rattled around the bend and then finally slowed down. I could hear the screeching of the brakes.

There was a frozen latte and an empty sandwich box. I looked around for a bin but I couldn't find one. I stared out at the clouds.

I really hate these desks because someone always asks if they can sit opposite you. But today felt different. I wanted someone to share the desk with. I felt chilled from the breeze and I stood up to shut the window.

I was supposed to start applications for a new job. I hated what I did for a living. I really hate marketing. I needed a new job to take my mind off things. I didn't want to stay at home and get high all day. I wanted to take a flight to Paris. Go on a holiday. I haven't gone anywhere in ages. I wondered what my ex was doing. Maybe she was out at a party or with friends. I wanted to phone her, but my days felt empty. I missed speaking to her. Doctor Addison's voice sounded exactly like hers.

I should probably tell my ex that my grandmother had passed away. We met up for coffee at Waterloo station a few days before it happened. Next time I will tell her but we haven't spoken since. I guess I am waiting for her to ask me how I am doing. I wish that I had a time machine. I want to go back and change how I left things with her.

I have not shaved in days. I went and got a haircut. I wanted to go for a bike ride at Richmond park but by the time I got home and showered, it was too late. So I delayed the ride until the following morning.

I felt very energetic and did not know what to do with myself. I took the bus to the gym in Kingston. I had not gone in months. My monthly membership was wasting away but I would never cancel it. I like having the choice to go there.

After leaving the gym, I felt very pleased with myself. I couldn't stop thinking about Doctor Addison. She was perfect. She was intelligent and beautiful.

Today I noticed how she had dressed down a bit. During our first session, she dressed way too sexy. I couldn't think straight but this morning she was more professional and seemed more down to earth. She seemed more nurturing.

I bet that all of her patients fall hard for her. I am just another patient to her. One of many. I really needed to stop thinking about her like that. She was there to do a job. I think that I should put the moves on her. What have I got to lose? I can always change to another Doctor.

I don't owe her anything so I think that I will just go for it. But first I will get in shape. Today was the first day after a long time that I felt as though I did not need to take any drugs or have a drink. Being sober felt like I was on a drug. I was riding the high of nothing which at that time felt like a high.

It felt good pouring out my soul without feeling judged. In a way, it felt like I had somebody on my side. Someone who could help me defeat this fear. A real professional.

Doctor Addison was not a clockwatcher. Our last 2 sessions ran over our time and she did not mention it. I hope that she doesn't bill me. I am going to stay quiet and not mention it to her. I liked how her eyebrows would furrow whenever she was trying to concentrate. It was really cute.

I felt very comfortable talking to Doctor Addison. I wished that I could talk to her all the time. She doesn't talk too much. Her face was utterly expressionless. Just the occasional prompt or nod. I wanted to ask her about herself without it looking like I am hitting on her.

The night was setting in. I decided to ride my bike early tomorrow morning. I turned over on my side, thinking it would be a long time before I fell asleep and then sleep rolled over me in a smooth dark wave and if anyone came in to peer on me while I slept, I would not have known it.

The following morning, I went to Richmond park. I rode my bicycle to the far end. I was riding my bike parallel to the river. I sat down in the shade beneath the tree, thinking of the unfilled days ahead, remembering my ex's face when she said goodbye to me.

I left my bike outside the corner shop on Park Road. I was going to buy a pack of cigarettes but I changed my mind at the very last minute. I bought a bottle of water and a protein bar instead.

I was still hungry and I was craving eggs. My ex used to bring me brown bread, eggs and avocado for breakfast on most mornings. I dropped off my bicycle at home and walked to the pub opposite the bicycle shop near Surbiton station. I ordered breakfast and a glass of orange juice.

I decided to call Doctor Max Weinberg. I told him about my dependency on Ketamine and how I read that it was used to treat depression.

'I am not super familiar with Ketamine other than knowing that it is being studied heavily right now and looks to show great promise in treating depression including treatment resistant depression,' explained Doctor Weinberg. 'Long-term efficiency studies are not comparable to SSRIs. There is far less research supporting it's safety and treatment potential.'

'What about using drugs and alcohol to help deal with PTSD?' I asked.

'I absolutely believe that someone could use drugs, alcohol and pretty much any other distraction (healthy or unhealthy) to cope with PTSD,' he said. 'As you probably know, those coping mechanisms just mask things and ultimately create more worry and regret than long-term relief.'

I said thank you to Doctor Weinberg and hung up. Maybe I should just stick with him and sack off Doctor Addison. It would work out much cheaper. I decided that I will stick with both of them. Doctor Weinberg was a professional Doctor and a licensed clinical social worker working in cardiovascular medicine. He was also a Certified Trauma Professional and had helped hundreds of people experiencing health trauma and PTSD.

Doctor Addison

Monday 9th February 2015

Morning

Amar was waiting in the reception room. He was flicking through a men's health magazine. When I first saw him, I thought that he looked healthier. He had a haircut, his beard was trimmed and he had a very neat stubble.

He looked excited and said that he had remembered something that he thought that he had forgotten forever. I invited him into my office and he took a seat on my couch.

'What is it?' I asked.

'I was walking home yesterday when two dogs barked at me. When I got home it must have triggered my memory. I forgot it almost straight away after the night of the 5th,' he took a deep breath and closed his eyes. 'I can picture my mother and both of my sisters crying.'

'Why were they crying?' I asked.

'They were crying because our dogs had their throats slit.'

'How did this happen?' I asked.

'I don't know. My mother went out to feed them and she found them both dead. My uncle buried our dogs at the back of our house,' explained Amar.

'How many dogs did you have?' I asked.

'We had 2. Their names were Toby and Tuc Tuc and they were both labradors. Toby protected the house and Tuc Tuc would protect our cars. He followed our car everywhere. One day, my uncle needed to borrow my father's car and Tuc Tuc barked at him and would not let him in.'

A tear ran down Amar's cheek and I handed him a box of tissues.

'Do you think that the two are linked?' I asked.

Amar looked very upset. He wiped away his tears.

'They had to be,' said Amar. 'In Montagne Blanche everyone keeps a lot of dogs.'

'Why is that?' I asked.

'To protect the family from anything bad. In our culture, dogs frighten away ghosts and evil spirits.'

Amar wiped his tears and spoke, 'I loved our dogs. Our house was newly built. We had a large guava tree in the garden and we used to all play underneath it. We even had a small pond surrounded by stone altars and shrines of hindu Gods and I can picture our two dogs playing in the pond and splashing water everywhere. It's strange how I forgot that we even had any dogs until recently,' he said.

'Who do you think could have done all of this?' I asked.

'I always thought that some deranged lunatic watched over our family. At first, he got rid of the dogs and then he came for us,' Amar said. 'Maybe it was somebody poor. Our family was well off and my father had a good job.'

'Would you ever go back and find out the truth for yourself?' I asked.

'Not a day goes by that I don't think about going back. I just want to know the truth. But I guess maybe deep down, the truth scares me,' he said.

'I can't blame you,' I replied.

'Tell me a little about yourself?' asked Amar.

'I graduated with a degree in psychology, a postgraduate certificate in applied systemic theory, a Masters in counselling psychology and a PHD in psychology and have been working out of my own practice for over 4 years in

Waterloo. I really enjoy my work but I dreamt of being a successful author ever since I was 5,' I said.

'I think that it's great that you have a dream,' said Amar.

Amar had been very inquisitive about my personal life and this was normal but I tried to sway the focus back over to him.

'Are you married?' he asked awkwardly.

I hadn't thought of a convincing lie. 'No, but I am engaged?' I said.

'When's the wedding?'

'We haven't set a date yet,' I replied.

I thought that Amar was exhibiting characteristics of transference neurosis. This takes place when the patient is transferring feelings he has onto the Doctor. With the Doctor's help, the patient can come to grips with this pattern, put his distortions into perspective and move on with his life. Amar was transferring emotional issues he had from his ex and grandmother on to me. He wished that his ex was still around to support him. He wished that he had told her the truth about his past. He wished that he had more time with his grandmother.

Amar smiled less and gave less of him. He barely looked at me. I took my time studying him. It was as though he was holding back from the session. He kept checking his wristwatch. We still had plenty of time left.

'Tell me more about your ex?' I asked.

'We lived together in Surbiton for over five years but we were never truly right for each other. She had changed to a completely different person by the end of the relationship,' he said.

'People sometimes grow apart,' I said. 'Maybe it was for the best.'

'I just wished that I had someone to face this with,' he said.

'Why did you break up?' I asked.

'We went to Milan for her birthday. Our hotel had bed bugs. We started arguing. The arguments were personal and we both said things that we regretted. When we got back to London, she packed her bags and moved out of our flat. She even took the cat. We decided to remain friends and stay in touch,' explained Amar. 'We still meet up for coffee at Waterloo station.'

'Do you want to get back together with her?' I asked.

'No,' he replied. 'Maybe if she changed back to the girl I once fell in love with five years ago but she is too different. The girl I was once in love with doesn't exist anymore. That shivery feeling is missing. It is totally gone. It was there once a long time ago but had now passed.'

Amar was still deeply affected from the break up. He said that the last 5 years would have been stale and colorless without her. He was dealing with a lot of issues all at once. His grandmother recently passed away. His girlfriend left him and his family were killed when he was five. Our session had come to an end.

I said goodbye and Amar left my office. He was rushing to leave without confirming our next session. I asked my assistant Sophie to call him later on to confirm our next appointment.

Amar

Monday 9th February 2015

Afternoon

I left Doctor Addison's office feeling upset. I did not know why I felt that way. Speaking with her had rekindled those lost feelings I had for my ex that I had pushed down. I could feel it suddenly resurfacing.

I stood at Embankment bridge and lit a cigarette. The cigarette had burned too quickly and I had another one straight away. The pain felt solid and heavy and sat in the middle of my chest. I didn't feel like going home which wasn't a good idea. I wished that I said something to her but the words kept evaporating, vanishing off my tongue.

It was windy and my lighter jammed but I managed to get it lit. I thought about going back to the gym or cooking something healthy but I was bored and I had run out of drugs. I flushed all my drugs away in the toilet this morning before leaving my house.

Fuck this new start. This new me. The minute you take a positive step in your life, you get knocked right back on your ass. I really needed a drink. I decided to walk to the casino in Leicester square to grab something to eat. I ordered a whisky and coke and looked at the menu. I wasn't hungry. I thought back to the last time I finished off a whole bottle of Jameson Irish whiskey to myself. There was nothing that I wanted to eat. The waiter returned and asked if I was ready. I ordered a beer and took the elevator up to the poker room on the fourth floor.

I messaged my friend Ray and told him that I was at the casino. I hadn't seen him in weeks. He was really there for me when me and my ex first broke up back in January. We spent a lot of time at the casinos in Leicester Square. Ray drinks but he has never touched any drugs. He was a fun companion to have at the casino.

I enjoyed playing roulette and blackjack but my problem was that I seldom won. My luck was better with poker. My tactic was to go all in and then double up if I lost. All I needed was one big win and then I would walk away but we all know how hard it is to walk away.

Ray messaged me back. Turns out he was already at the bottom floor of the Hippodrome casino. I took the lift down to meet him. He knew I was having trouble in my life lately. He was trying to cheer me up but he was busy placing his chips on the roulette table. He bought me a drink.

I thought back to all the times I had come here with my ex. One time we watched a tribute band to "The Rat Pack." The singers looked nothing like Frank Sinatra and Dean Martin. I think they got a mexican to play Sammy Davis Jr but once they started to sing they absolutely nailed it.

During the intermission, I went downstairs and played a hand of no limit texas hold'em. I went all in on the second hand. This guy came in with me. Luckily I won it on the river. I had doubled my money. We returned back to the show and had missed the first few minutes. I looked at the menu and ordered a rat pack manhattan. It was a special cocktail to coincide with the show.

I got tickets for a cabaret show here at the Hippodrome on my ex's birthday a few years ago and another time we saw a tribute band for Stevie Wonder which wasn't very good.

I was still upset from my session with Doctor Addison but I felt like we were making progress. I felt the sleepless nights coming. My heart felt like a flutter in my chest, like a bird trying to get out of a cage. It was around 7:30 pm and there were strangers on their way home from work.

That afternoon, I spent over 5 hours at the casino. At first, it was fun and I was up. I took a break and walked around the corner to Chinatown. I went to my favorite restaurant on the strip. After I ate, I decided to go home but then I remembered how empty my flat was. There was nothing waiting for me except for my television and books. I wasn't drunk enough. I was up and should have just gone home but I went back and kept on gambling. I ended up losing all the money that I had just won and a lot more.

I spend too much time in my head. I was very upset and then from out of nowhere, I gained clarity. Losing all that money made me forget all about the Doctor and my ex. Doctor Addison was a complete professional which was what I needed. I just wished that I could touch her or kiss her.

I was very drunk and wanted to let go. I wanted to disappear. I did not want to exist. I promised myself yesterday that I wasn't going to touch any drugs but that was all that I wanted. I called my dealer several times but his phone went to voicemail.

It was raining. The headlights of passing cars blurred the wet pavement. I stood there a long time gazing at the rain swept streets staring for hours at the rain. It felt like my body would fall loose, shaking free of the world of reality. I always believed that rain had the power to hypnotize.

I stopped at an off license and bought a bottle of Jameson Irish Whisky. I went home and drank myself into oblivion until I passed out. I felt like I was breathing through a mask. It hurt as if a small hole had opened up in my heart.

Rain continued to fall without a sound. Every single window in my flat was open yet it still felt airless and I couldn't stop replaying the scene. I felt as though I was back there. That night all those years ago when my world was ripped apart.

Doctor Addison

Morning

I went out in the receptionist room. Amar was not here and had not called to say that he would be running late. I wondered if he was going to show up. 30 minutes had passed. I had the next 2 hours allocated for our session. I should not have said that I was engaged.

Amar should have been in therapy years ago or maybe now was the right time for him. I think that he feels that he cannot run away from his problems any longer.

I was sat at my desk and reading the Metro newspaper. Sometimes this newspaper is filled with really informative content and sometimes its just filled with bullshit. I don't think I have gone a single day without picking up a copy. I had given up smoking for the past 6 months and staring out into the empty couch gave me an urge to pop out for a cigarette.

My phone rang and my receptionist Sophie informed me that Amar had arrived. I went to greet him.

'I'm sorry that I'm late,' he said. 'I didn't sleep at all last night and I missed my alarm this morning.'

'That's alright,' I said. 'We can start the session now if you are ready.'

Amar thanked me and took a seat on my couch. He looked pale and his breath still reeked of alcohol.

'How are you?' I asked.

'I could be better,' he replied. 'I'm a little hungover.'

He explained how after our last session, he went to the Hippodrome casino in Leicester square for a drink and ended up gambling for over 6 hours.

'Sounds like fun,' I joked.

'It was fun,' he replied. 'When I left the casino I phoned my dealer to pick up but he didn't reply. My period of sobriety didn't last as long as I'd hoped.'

'Thank you for being honest,' I said.

'You have helped me a lot but I was wondering if maybe you can recommend another Doctor,' suggested Amar.

'What's the matter?' I asked.

'I have been speaking to another psychiatrist over the telephone because I wanted a second opinion,' said Amar. 'During our last session you asked me if it was okay to use me for a case study. I asked you if my name would be mentioned. You said that it would remain completely anonymous. The other Doctor said that case studies are a less common form of research, but certainly still being done. He said that this is a more common practice for psychiatrists that also have dual appointments doing research, but not for your average psychiatrist. He said that he was sure that your research would give great consideration and care for me and my outcome.'

'So what's the problem?' I asked.

Amar took a deep breath.

'He said that if I thought that my psychiatrist reminded me of someone in a negative way then that would be a good reason to find another Doctor. He told me to trust my instincts when it came to getting therapy. He explained that the match and connectedness with that person is the bedrock of my progress and any reason standing in the way of that click is good enough to justify termination,' realiterated Amar.

I am sorry to hear that Amar,' I said. 'Who do I remind you of?'

'I'd rather not say,' replied Amar.

Amar could not face me.

'I guess you have a right to know,' he said. 'It's my ex. You remind me of her. You have that same voice. You are both warm and comforting. I just think that it would be easier with somebody else. Another Doctor may be able to treat me without rekindling those emotions.'

I explained to Amar how I thought that he was exhibiting characteristics of transference neurosis.

He asked me what it was and I explained how he was projecting the image of his ex on to me and that this was quite normal.

'Deep down you want your ex to be here by your side and to support you through this difficult period. But you have not told her about your grandmother's passing or anything about your family's past,' I said. 'I think that as long as you are making progress then we should not terminate our sessions.'

I urged Amar to have a few more sessions with me. Amar looked like his decision was already made. I could not risk losing him. I teared up a piece of paper out of my notepad, wrote my phone number on it and handed it over to him.

'Amar that is my personal line,' I said. 'I want you to call me if you feel that you need to. Your case is very serious and I don't think that you should change Doctor. I really hate the fact that you are facing this alone, especially so soon after your grandmother had just passed.'

'Alright. You have convinced me,' he replied.

'I had a strange dream last night,' said Amar.

'About what?' I asked.

'There was a little girl and she was playing with my sisters toys,' he said.

'I want you to write down all of your dreams in a journal. They could be memories from your past. Are you planning on going back to Mauritius?' I asked.

'I'm not sure,' he said. 'I'll take a look at flights tonight when I get home.'

'I want you to phone me anytime that you feel that you need to. I am fully aware that you are facing this nightmare all alone and I want you to know that I am here to support you professionally,' I said.

Amar thanked me. He said goodbye and went back out into the waiting room.

Amar

Thursday 12th February 2015

Afternoon

I left Doctor Addison's office. Just before I left, I noticed studious notes in her slovenly handwriting about her patients. Maybe it was about me. I wanted to read what she'd written but I didn't have enough time.

I could not stop thinking about the dream that I had last night. I wondered what it meant. I wondered what else my mind had suppressed. My dreams are becoming more frequent or are they visions of my past. Fragments of my memory.

I stood at Embankment bridge and watched as the boats passed by below me. There was a large white boat and it looked like they were having a party. I got out my box of cigarettes. I smoked one and decided to keep the rest for later.

I walked slowly to platform 8 and boarded the train home. I stopped off at Waitrose and bought some groceries. I wanted to buy another pack of cigarettes but the queue was too long.

My grandmother and my ex were lost to me forever. I thought about leaving London. I can't stay here any longer. I needed a change. I felt like the hands of a clock running in only one direction. The years of disappointment, loneliness and silence was finally settling in my mind.

I withdrew into myself. I ate alone. I walked alone. I gambled alone. I went to the movies alone. I started talking to myself and I drank alone at night.

I contacted Doctor Weinberg. I told him that Doctor Addison had given me her personal phone number. She wanted me to call her in case of an emergency.

'I want to know if this may be breaching any ethical lines between a Doctor and a patient?' I said.

'It really varies,' explained Doctor Weinberg. 'However, if she is a trauma specialist or handles patients who may be more at risk, then yes, allowing patients access to her for emergencies during off hours is not uncommon. It actually could be part of a patient's safety plan but boundaries around this should probably be more thoroughly discussed than "call me anytime." Not exactly the "norm" but not unethical or inappropriate.'

It turns out Doctor Addison was not overstepping any boundaries. Deep down I was hoping that she was. I thought that I was different to her other patients. I still can't stop thinking about her. A woman like that would never be interested in a guy like you. I wish that I was more like her. She had ambitions and dreams. I loved how she dreamt of being a famous author. I am going to think of clever things to say to impress her.

I unlocked the door to my flat. There was rubbish everywhere. I had not cleaned my living room properly in months.

I searched the internet for flights to Mauritius. They were too expensive. Flying from London to Mauritius is never cheap. Maybe I should go in a few months time. I decided to have another smoke. I know that if I stayed here in London, something inside me would be lost forever. Something that I couldn't afford to lose.

I wish that the police would just call me and say that they have found the killer. I have waited all these years and I guess I'm still waiting. Deep down I was still afraid. That whole act in front of the Doctor was just for show. I don't think that I am ready to go back.

I cleaned my flat. I found a pile of unopened letters. It was probably unpaid bills and fines that had accumulated. I skimmed through the pile. I noticed a letter enclosed in a creme envelope. It looked hand written. I opened the letter. It was from my grandmother.

Doctor Addison

Morning

I arrived at work early that morning. I sat down and sipped my coffee. I replied to a few emails and after I read my copy of the Metro. I skimmed past the horoscopes section and instead of reading it, I quickly turned the page so I didn't catch a glimpse of my horoscope. I don't believe in any of it but I'd rather go through my day not knowing. Horoscopes can be spot on whether it's about relationships or related to work. I hated it and found it quite daunting so I'd rather not know.

I haven't had any fun in quite some time now. The thing is that I am saving up for a mortgage. I have most of the money saved up. I really hate renting in London. Every month I am paying for somebody else's mortgage. I detested the middle pages of the Metro newspaper. All I see is fancy flats that I will never be able to afford. I hope that one day I can write a really successful book. I'll buy a really nice townhouse or a barge with the money. The money would be nice and hopefully I will be able to write full time. Thrillers are very popular. They just fly off the shelves. Maybe one day I will write something in that capacity.

My assistant Sophie came in with my coffee and I asked her if we had any cancellations.

'No,' she replied.

Sophie informed me that Amar had arrived. I was curious to find out what he needed to tell me. I invited him into my office before our session was due to start. He walked inside. He was sharply dressed and looked well rested.

He took a seat on my couch.

'I found this letter,' he said.

'Who is it from?' I asked.

'It's from my grandmother,' he replied. 'She must have posted it before she passed away.'

'Have you read it?' I asked.

'I read it last night?' replied Amar.

'Can I read it?' I asked.

'Yes, go ahead,' he said.

I put on my reading glasses.

I read it over twice.

'Why didn't you phone me?' I asked.

'I wanted to tell you about it in person,' Amar said. 'In the letter, she explained that one day she would like me to return to Mauritius to scatter her ashes. I have already booked flights to Mauritius for tomorrow.'

'I don't think that she meant so soon. Do you think that you are ready?' I asked.

'I am probably never going to be ready but I don't want to wait any longer,' said a determined Amar. 'Søren Kierkegaard wrote that "Life can only be understood backwards; but it must be lived forwards."

'I love his book fear and trembling. Amar you should think of a plan,' I suggested.

'I'm going to speak to the local police,' he said. 'Maybe I can get them to reopen the case.'

'But it was a long time ago?' I said. 'Amar. I want you to phone me and update me on everything.'

'Maybe you should come with me?' He suggested.

I paused and checked to see if he was being serious.

'Maybe I'll meet you down there,' I said. 'I'm only joking. I don't think that it's a good idea. It's not very professional.'

'Who cares,' he said. 'Mauritius is a beautiful country and we can hang out at the beach.'

'I'll think about it,' I said. 'Good luck.'

Amar shook my hand.

I leaned in and hugged him.

'Good luck,' I said.

'Thanks,' he replied. 'What are you reading?' He pointed to my book.

'Death in the afternoon,' I said. 'It's by Hemingway.'

'What's it about?' he asked.

'It's a book about bullfighting,' I replied.

'Is it any good?'

'Way better than I expected,' I said.

'Have you read The happy short life of Francis Macomber?' asked Amar. 'It's also written by Hemingway. It's about a hunter.'

'No,' I replied. 'I will definitely check it out. Thank you. I'll add it to my reading list.'

'Goodbye,' he said.

Amar left

Amar

Monday 16th February 2015

Afternoon

I wanted to have a quick smoke at Embankment bridge but I didn't want to miss my train. The next one was in 20 minutes. A copy of the metro newspaper was folded into the gap next to my seat. I took it out and glanced at the sports section at the back.

I still haven't packed. I can probably buy whatever I needed out there. I checked my wristwatch. It was 5pm which meant that it was 1pm in Mauritius. I'll have to keep that in mind whenever I phone Doctor Addison. I thought about how this may bring us closer together. Maybe she will fall in love with me. I noticed how her small earrings glittered at her hair.

I went to Waitrose near Surbiton station. I know without looking at my watch that it was nearly 6pm.

Doctor Addison called.

'You should hire a Private Investigator to assist you while you are out there,' she said.

'Can you have a look on the internet for me?' I asked.

'Sure, I'll have a look,' replied Doctor Addison.

I went out onto the balcony and had a cigarette. I noticed the old man watching the television. I could see an image of myself in him. An old man dying all alone. I didn't want to go out like that. I don't want to die alone and full of regrets. I chipped out the rest of my cigarette and went back inside. I looked at my empty flat. I can't believe she took the cat with her. We named our cat Norah Jones after the singer. I miss our cat. I am all alone. She should have left the cat with me.

I wrote a note for my neighbours. I didn't know them that well. There was a Japanese girl who lived next door. She was studying at Kingston University. She was friends with my ex back when she used to live here. She used to bring us left over sushi from the restaurant that she worked at.

My other neighbour was a coke addict named Craig. He was a little crazy. I didn't want to be friends with him. I always tried to avoid running into him. He tried to borrow money off me a few times. I think that he still owes my ex around £600. I wanted to ask him for it but I heard that he was fired from his last 3 jobs. I kinda felt sorry for him.

The note read that I was going away for a month or so and to call me in case of an emergency.

I did not pack a lot but I made sure I had my passport and boarding pass. I lied down and closed my eyes.

I woke up. My morning breath warmed the pillow. Today was not a day for second guessing or regret, it was a day for doing. I understood that my days in this sleepy town were numbered. I yearned for change. My heart and body craved for the answers to my past. I wished that Doctor Addison could accompany me to Mauritius. It would be fun having her around. Maybe we would grow closer together. It could be a fun adventure. I am certain that this is probably unethical. I remembered how I thought that her giving me her private number was unethical. I decided to call Doctor Weinberg.

I asked him if a Doctor was allowed to accompany a patient back to the place of trauma to help them overcome their PTSD.

'I think that this is not unethical but I feel that this may be a more advanced part of therapy for trauma,' explained Doctor Max Weinberg. 'Being in this setting could re-trigger you so you would have to be certain that you have already been given the tools and training to cope with the strong feelings that may arise before trying to elicit them through this experience. Patients who are forced to confront their trauma before they are properly trained are at greater risk for going back in progress, not forward.'

'Is there a name for this?' I asked.

'This is called "in vivo exposure" and it is an ethical treatment. You are not side-stepping any boundaries. In real life, therapy often has to involve real-world experiences as opposed to more sterile office encounters,' explained Doctor Weinberg.

'Thank you,' I said.

Amar

Tuesday 17th February 2015

Morning

I arrived at the airport. The lady at the helpdesk said that my flight from London Gatwick to Sir Seewoosagur Ramgoolam International airport should take around 12 hours.

I still had some drugs tucked away in my wallet. I needed to get rid of it. I locked myself in the toilet cubicle and searched my wallet. I found a bag of ketamine and cocaine. The bags were about half full. I rubbed a little bit of it into my gums before I flushed it away.

'Goodbye,' I said.

I read somewhere that because of the lower levels of oxygen in your blood, you may seem more drunk in the air than you would on the ground after consuming the same amount of alcohol, which meant that I can drink myself into a nice little cocoon.

I went past the final security check and I was waiting to board the plane at my gate. I don't understand why people queue up just before you are about to board the plane. My friend told me about a trick that you can use to get on the plane before everybody else. The trick is to walk to the front of the queue and tell them that you have a peanut allergy and that you need to wipe the seat down thoroughly. I don't know if it actually works and I have never tried it. One day I will see. I didn't want to get seated near a baby or an annoying kid. All that crying and shouting for 12 hours would drive me insane.

I boarded the plane. I wondered how long I should wait before I can ask the stuartist for a drink. I was counting down the seconds. I couldn't wait any longer.

'Excuse me miss,' I said. 'I'm feeling a little nervous for you see it's my first time flying. I was wondering if maybe you could fetch me a drink.'

'Sure what do you want?' asked the stuartist.

'Have you got any rum?'

'Sure I'll have that over to you straight away,' she said.

The plane ascended up into the sky and I started to drift away.

I woke up and checked my wristwatch. I tried to calculate how long I was asleep for. My personal television indicated that we would land in 10 hours. I realised that only 2 hours had passed. I wished that I had been asleep for longer.

I thought back to when I took my first ever flight with my grandmother to London. Back then, planes were very different. They were much larger, louder and less comfortable. That was my first ever time on a plane and I can remember how I played Ludo with my grandmother.

I closed my eyes and thought about Sir Seewoosagur Ramgoolam International Airport. There was a deck area where you can watch the planes take off. The area had a brown glass case around it and I wondered if it was still there.

My flight took a little longer to land but I was in no rush to get out. The other passengers grabbed their luggage and were all queuing up to leave. Everyone was rushing to get off the plane. A stewardess tapped me on my shoulder.

'We have landed sir. Do you need any help with your luggage?' She asked.

'No, I'll be fine,' I said. 'Thank you miss.'

I walked towards passport control.

I decided to keep my head down and lay low. I wanted to ask my uncle if I could stay at his place but I decided to stay at a hotel instead. My grandmother wrote in her letter that I should not trust anyone, even close family members. Maybe it was for the best.

As soon as I landed it felt like a blast of fresh air. I breathed an air of ineffable sweetness.

I walked out of the airport and looked for a taxicab stand.

Doctor Addison

Tuesday 17th February 2015

Afternoon

Amar messaged me to say that he had landed safely.

I called him back.

'I met a taxi driver,' Amar said. 'His name is Dev. He drove me to my hotel in Port Louis. He recommended that I visit the waterfront. I asked him where he was from and Dev said that he lived in Montagne Blanche with his wife and two kids. What are the chances?'

'I'm sure that it's just a coincidence,' I replied. 'Did you ask him if he knew anything about the murder from over 20 years ago?'

'I was going to but I decided that I did not want to broach the subject,' said Amar. 'The traffic leading into Port Louis was really bad. I got impatient and decided to walk. My suitcase was not heavy and I had packed really light. I got out and said goodbye. Dev handed me his card and said to call him if I needed a cab back to the airport. I dragged my suitcase on the pavement all the way to the reception area of my hotel. The hotel was located in the heart of the city. It was called the Grand Hotel. I picked this hotel specifically because there was 24 hour CCTV security cameras, a security guard and it was located near a police station.'

'Good idea,' I said.

'I still haven't unpacked. Have you thought about what I asked you?' said Amar. 'My grandmother left me money for her funeral and there is some money left over. I'll pay for your flights and hotel. You can help me investigate. It will be strictly professional and part of the in-vivo exposure process.'

'I'm not sure,' I said. 'I need a little more time to think about it.' I told Amar to get plenty of sleep and that he had a big day ahead of him. 'What will you do tomorrow?'

'I am going to take a taxi to Montagne Blanche. I want to see if I can remember anything,' he said.

'Are you going to return to the crime scene?' I asked.

'No. I don't think so,' said Amar. 'I'm not ready. I just want to get a feel of what the town is like.'

'I think that you should try and solve this case without ever stepping foot at the crime scene,' I said.

'I agree,' said Amar. 'If I am being totally honest, I don't think that I will ever be ready to step foot back inside that house.'

'That's fine,' I said. 'I understand and if I were in your shoes, I would be exactly the same.'

I said goodbye and hung up the phone.

I was getting ready to leave my practice. I told Amar to call me tomorrow morning. I had a lot of paperwork to complete and Sophie had left early today. I was the last person to leave. I had to make sure that I locked up properly.

I crossed Embankment bridge and listened to a guy playing a trumpet. He was really good and so I gave him all the change that I had in my purse. I hung around Southbank. It was cold but bearable. I walked all the way to Trafalgar Square and then back to Waterloo station.

I was too tired to cook and so I ordered a Pizza. I turned off the television and decided to write but I needed some inspiration. I lived in a rented flat at Raynes Park.

I fell on my creaking bed which I needed to replace. I thought I heard an intruding noise that woke me up. My pulse started racing. It was probably just my imagination. I hated living alone. I decided to read until I felt sleepy.

Amar

Wednesday 18th February 2015

Morning

The curtain was slightly drawn and the lights had hit my
eyes. I was deep in a dream. It was a wonderful dream
about a happier time with my family. The lovely dream
faded into a nightmare. It suddenly came over me like a
wave of black dread. I ran my hands across my hair and
felt a bump. My hair was matted with blood. I started
breathing deeply, trying to slow down my heart rate. I
woke up from a dream in a pool of my sweat. My
nightmares were getting worse. It's like it consumes me
and part of me just wants to forget it and then the other part
just wants to try and remember. I am terrified of what will
happen if I ever do. It feels like I am far away looking at
myself.

   I managed to wake up before my alarm went off. I took a
shower and thought about Montagne Blanche. I closed my
eyes and let the warm water massage the top of my head.

   I tried to picture what my home town looked like. I
remembered how we lived at the top of a road called
Chemier Boulangerie. Chemier means road in french.
There was the main road that had a parade a shops
including a supermarket, two hairdressers opposite each
other, a chinese restaurant and a shop that sold sarees. On
the opposite side of the street there was a VHS shop.

Further down the road, there was a pharmacy and a small park with swings and a roundabout. I can remember a lemonade stand.

I decided to see what else I could remember. There was something disturbing about recalling a warm memory and feeling utterly cold. I closed my eyes and recalled a primary school and at the very bottom of that road was a dental practice. My mother took me there once and I had an injection into my gums. That was my first ever visit to the dentist.

I wanted to see what else I could remember. I closed my eyes and I could hear the sound of my mother's voice. She was saying goodbye to my two sisters moments before they got on their school bus.

My mind started to drift. I saw flashes of my sister's dead bodies. I tried not to think about it but my mind was fixated.

I got out of the shower and dried myself. I took the elevator down into the lobby of the hotel and decided to skip breakfast. I went out for a cigarette.

I called Dev and asked him to pick me up from my hotel. It was a few minutes after midday and the sky was cloudless. Dev said that he can pick me up in an hour. He sounded confused because I asked him to take me to Montagne Blanche. I told him that I would explain everything to him in person. I hated explaining things over the telephone.

The car arrived. I got in.

'Why do you want to go to Montagne Blanche?' he asked.

'I have to visit a friend,' I said.

'What's his name?' asked Dev.

'I don't think that you know him,' I replied. 'What is the town like?'

'It's a small town, very quiet, between Flacque and Moka district.'

'Why is it called Montagne Blanche?' I asked.

'There is a mountain and sometimes when it is very cold, the top of it is snow capped,' he replied.

A flurry of rain fell over the road. I stared out of the car window and it got very windy. The rain had come from out of nowhere. My heart started racing and I started to feel trepidation. The rain made me feel trapped and I felt like I was breathing through a mask. I wanted the rain to stop. It was hard to see clearly out of the car window. The windscreen wipers were batting back and forth and screeching against the car windows.

A road sign indicated that Montagne Blanche was in a few kilometres. Everything had slowed down and I couldn't breath.

'Can we turn around please?' I said with laboured breathing.

'Why?' asked Dev.

'I forgot something back at the hotel,' I said. 'I need to go back and quickly grab it.'

'Are you sure?' he said. 'We are almost there.'

'Yes. Turn the car around now,' I said.

'Okay my friend. Don't have a heart attack. I need to find somewhere safe to turn,' he said. 'Are you sure that you are okay?'

'What do you mean?' I said.

'You look like you have just seen a ghost,' said Dev.
'Can I ask you a question?'

'What is it?' I said.

'Is your name Amar? Did you move to London after your family got killed?' asked Dev.

'How do you know that?' I asked him.

'I searched your surname in to google last night. I saw it in the newspapers from a few years ago,' explained Dev. 'I knew that I recognised it from somewhere. They still mention it in the local newspapers.'

'Can you please not tell anyone that I am here?' I asked.
Dev said nothing.

'Okay how much do you want?' I pleaded. 'I'll give you 2000 rupees. I am only going to be here for a few weeks. Once I have done what I came here to do, you can tell whoever you want.'

'How come you decided to come back?' he asked.

'I came here to find out the truth,' I said.

'What if the killer comes after you?' asked Dev.

'I don't care. I am tired of hiding,' I replied. 'What does the house look like nowadays?'

'It's a big house, long driveway, abandoned. After what happened no one goes anywhere near it. The townspeople think that it's haunted or cursed. I drove past it a few times and it was in a bad shape. Its been through a lot of cyclones. The roof is barely holding up. Even the road leading up to the house is covered with branches and vines. Do you want some advice?' he said rhetorically. 'I think that you should just go back to London. Finding the killer is not going to bring your family back.'

'I'm here because I want to know the truth. I want to hire a Private Investigator. Do you know anyone?' I asked.

'Check the internet,' replied Dev.

We finally arrived at the town. We drove near the mountain and I noticed how the top of it was not snow capped. I noticed a crow etching a circle into the sky. The rain had calmed but it was still wet. I started looking around and noticed a cinema. It all started coming back to me. I went there once and watched an animated film called Jungle Jack with my parents and sisters.

We drove past a supermarket called Baby Dollar Store. I remembered that supermarket from when I was little. My mother would get her groceries from there.

The rain had stopped and the sun started to rise up from out of the clouds. The town had changed considerably and there were new buildings. The town was dismal and cold. Much colder than Port Louis and the silence of the town had settled deep into my mind. There was hardly anyone around. Maybe because everyone was probably at work or at school. Everything had changed. Nothing was how I imagined it in my mind.

Dev stopped the car and pointed. 'Over in that direction is the road that takes you up to the abandoned house,' he explained.

I closed my eyes and I could instantly recapture the route that my father took home each night. The same way home now felt like a foreign town. I spotted more crows hovering over our car. My heart started racing.

'I'm not ready just yet,' I said to Dev. 'This is all too much to take in at once.'

'I understand,' he said. 'Do you want me to take you back to Port Louis?'

'Yes,' I replied.

On the journey back, I asked him if he could drive me around again tomorrow.

'I am very sorry,' he said. 'That house gives me the creeps, but I want you to call me if you need a lift to the airport. What will you do tomorrow?'

'I don't know,' I said.

I took out my wallet and handed 2000 rupees over to Dev. At first, he turned it away. I offered it again and he finally accepted. He promised that he would not tell anyone that I was here. I promised him another 2000 rupees if I uncovered the truth about my family.

He smiled.

I thanked him.

I returned back to my hotel and phoned Doctor Addison. I had no idea what tomorrow would bring but I was certain that I was not ready to go near the abandoned house. I needed someone to help me investigate. It was a shame that Dev was not available.

Doctor Addison

Wednesday 18th February 2015

Afternoon

I received a missed call from Amar and I wanted to call him back straight away but I was busy. I told him that I would call him back in a few hours. I was on my way to the Cafe Nero in Piccadilly Circus. It was situated on the opposite side of the giant Waterstones book store.

I go to a writer's group meet-up every wednesday to work on my writing. I found out about the group on a social media app. Its really cool. There are tons of social events set up for aspiring writers all over London.

I finished work early today. I decided to walk from Waterloo to Piccadilly Circus. The walk takes around 30 minutes. I crossed over to the other side of Embankment bridge. I was starving. I walked past a restaurant called Herman Ze German. I was craving a currywurst but my feet ached and I just wanted to get to the cafe and start writing.

I had reached Trafalgar Square. There were flocks of tourists all wearing the same red shirt. I tried to read the writing on the shirt but I couldn't see that far.

I walked past the Capital F.M radio station and then I took a left at Hippodrome casino. I kept on walking until I reached Piccadilly Circus tube station. I was waiting at the busy intersection for the lights to turn green.

I arrived over an hour early today. I ordered an espresso and a ham and cheese croissant. I took a seat at the far corner on the left. My laptop needed charging. I sat down and put my earphones on. I wasn't playing any music. I like to keep my earphones in my ear to drown out the noisy cafe.

There was a couple arguing in the seat next to mine. Her coffee untouched grew cold. The customer's umbrellas carried with them the scent of the chilly rain. Her hair was wet and strands were pressed to her forehead. Her fingers were still wet and chilled. I noticed how her fingers trembled slightly. I was glad that I arrived at the cafe before it started to rain.

I got a call from Amar but I didn't answer it. I sent him a text and asked if it was urgent. It wasn't. I said that I would call him back in a few hours.

I started writing a story about a boy that lost his family when he was five years old. I had written over 4,000 words in only two hours. The organiser of the writing group walked over to me.

'Hey are you joining us at the pub?' she asked.

'Not this time,' I said. 'I have to finish off this chapter but I will be there next week.'

She gathered the other members of the writing group and they walked to the pub to drink and to talk about literature. This writing group was pretty cool. I met a guy from America who directed documentaries. There was another filmmaker who made a film about a model who killed herself but generally you mostly meet aspiring authors looking to catch a break.

I needed a drink but I decided to skip the pub. I wanted to go home and phone Amar. I wanted to find out about his day so I can write about it. I got on at Green Park station and I took the tube all the way home to Raynes Park. I should have jumped on the overground at Waterloo. The other route is much quicker.

I walked into my flat and called Amar straight away. He sounded tired.

'So what happened today?' I asked.

'Dev drove me to Montagne Blanche and showed me around the town,' explained Amar. 'I dreamt of this place almost every night in my dreams but once I was actually there, everything was very different. In my heart, I knew deep down that this was the place where I first grew up and where my parents raised me. We stayed inside the car and I didn't get out even once. We stayed on the main road. We went near the road that lead up to the crime scene. I saw a crow perched on a branch leading into the road. Images of my family's bludgeoned bodies flashed before me. I asked Dev to turn the car around and he drove me back to my hotel.'

'I checked the internet and found a guy called Le Clezio who has established himself as the best Private Investigator working out of Port Louis,' I said. 'I have emailed you his information. Call him tomorrow morning to book an appointment.'

'Thanks,' replied Amar.

'Have you booked a return flight to London?' I asked.

'I paid for an open return ticket,' he said. 'You should fly down and help me investigate. We can be like Sherlock Holmes and Watson. I saw a copy of A Study in Scarlet on your desk. I can pay for your flights and hotel with the money that my grandmother left me. You can help me overcome the final step of my fear through in-vivo exposure.'

I said that I would try and make arrangements. We continued speaking over the telephone. I looked up and noticed the time. I had lost track of how long we had spoken for. I wanted to hang up but I wasn't feeling very sleepy.

Amar sent me a picture of Le Monde Brabant which is an underwater waterfall at sea.

'We can take a helicopter to look at it,' he said.

The picture was breathtaking and after we finished talking, I stayed up a little while longer googling more images of Mauritius. It looked like paradise.

Amar called me back.

'What should I say to the Detective?' he asked.

'We need him to revisit the crime scene and check whether the police may have missed any clues from the night of the murder,' I said. 'We also need to take a look at the police report from the night of 5th.'

I wanted the case solved without Amar having to set foot back at the crime scene. We were both hoping that it would not come to that.

'Stay at the hotel tonight. Don't get drunk and wander off into town,' I said.

When I spoke to Amar over the phone, I had a feeling that he had been drinking alone. Amar went on and on about a beer called Phoenix. He wished that they sold it in London. He also bought a whole case of red label whisky from a duty free store at the airport. Amar said that he drank to calm his nerves but I had a feeling that he was substituting the drugs with alcohol.

'Have you craved any drugs?' I asked.

'I want to stay focused and I think that the drugs are a distraction,' he explained. 'I didn't come here for that. I came here to find answers.'

I was feeling sleepy and had work early tomorrow morning.

I said goodnight and hung up the phone.

I couldn't fall asleep. I turned on my laptop and started writing. I was writing about Amar's case. I had written two different narratives. The first draft was non-fictional account of everything. The second draft was a fictional story. I sat by my laptop and thought about the ending. Will it be a happy ending or will it be a sad one? Will Amar find the killer or will the killer find him? Once I started writing, it started to pour out of me like I had just severed a vein.

Amar

Night

I drifted off to a restless sleep. I woke up in the middle of the night sensing that someone was in the hotel room with me. My heart was pounding. I quietly placed my hands on a golf club and stayed very still. I stood up slowly but stayed low and crouched. Flashes of a little girl.

I peered around as best I could in the semi darkness. I checked the bathroom and then the closets. I began to feel silly stalking the hotel room but I definitely heard a noise. I waited a few seconds before I flicked on the light just to be sure. I definitely heard a noise.

Had my nightmares drifted off into reality? Who was this young girl following me in my dreams? I think that I am losing my sense of reality. I could not sleep last night. I stayed awake thinking that somebody else was in the hotel room with me.

I fell in and out of sleep. I dreamt about Doctor Addison. I wish that I could just hold her in my arms.

I got up at 6am and went for a run on the beach. It felt like a storm was brewing. The constant sweep of the ocean breeze was a warning from the sea that it could pounce at any minute and engulf me. After my run, I had breakfast at the hotel's restaurant.

I phoned the Private Detective. His name was Jean Le Clezio. By the sound of his name, he was a Franco

Mauritian. I told him that I was staying in a hotel in Port Louis. He asked me to write down an address. He wanted me to meet him in 2 hours.

I spoke to the receptionist at my hotel. I said that if anyone comes looking for me to tell them that I will be at this address. It was the address that the Detective had given me. I decided to create a trail just in case I went missing.

I had trouble finding the place. The back streets were crowded and filthy. This part of the city was a stark contrast to the waterfront. My hotel was not far and so I walked there last night to stare at the boats.

The Private Detective's office was located at the top of a chinese restaurant. I took the dilapidated stairs up and knocked on a grey metallic door.

There was no answer. I decided to ring him.

He opened the door and invited me in.

'My name is Detective Le Clezio, you must be Tony,' he said.

I had given him a fake name.

I shook his hand.

He asked me to take a seat.

'How can I help you?' he said.

'I want you to find out everything about a family that was murdered a long time ago in Montagne Blanche. It was well documented in the newspapers.

I handed him a dossier on the case.

Detective Le Clezio had an aura of confidence and spoke english with a strong french accent. Art hung all around his office, pictures of gothic style buildings. I saw a picture of a young girl. Her family must have reported her missing. There was over 15 notice boards with information on other cases.

'I want a list of anything that you can think of. Check if the family may have owed money to someone. I want to know everything,' I said.

He nodded.

'I don't want the killer to suspect anything. When you are investigating do not mention me or indicate that there is someone interested in the case,' I explained.

'Okay,' he said.

'I want a video of the crime scene,' I said. 'I want you to capture the whole property and even the road leading up to it. Once you have it, can you please email it to me or put everything on this memory card.'

He smiled.

'How much do you think all of this is going to cost me?' I asked.

'I don't know yet,' he replied. 'I need to have a look first. I will call you later in the evening.'

'That's fine. What's the story behind your surname?' I asked.

'Have you ever read a book by an author named Jean-Marie Gustave Le Clézio?' asked the Detective.

'Yes,' I said. 'Wait you are not related to him are you?'

'Nope,' he said. 'I just like the name and I wanted to protect my identity. A Private Detective makes a lot of enemies.'

'I can only imagine,' I said.

I shook Detective Le Clezio's hand. His hands were rough. He said to wait by a telephone for his call.

I left his office and went to the chinese restaurant. I called Dev to ask if he wanted to come out for a beer. He said that he was working but maybe another time.

I slowly sipped my drink and thought about my old home. I remember chasing after our dogs in the garden. I played hide and seek with my sisters. Me and Neha used to hide in the closet. That was my favorite hiding place and turned out to be the place that saved me. She would hold my hands whenever we would cross the street. She was very clever. My sister Teha was the oldest. She was the bossy one. She always got her way and cried when she didn't. She always wanted all the attention.

One day Neha dared me to climb up a ledge and Teha grabbed me before I fell to any harm. Neha was usually the quiet one. She kept to herself. Neha reminded me of the girl following me in my dreams except her face was completely different. The only similarity was that they both carried the same creepy doll. I wish that the fragments of my memory would piece together. I can't make sense of anything.

One night, our two dogs started acting very strange. They chased after me and Neha and it looked like they wanted to hurt us both, but luckily Teha fended them off and they backed away until my mother came.

She tried to get the dogs to leave me and my sisters alone but they would not stop. It was like they were possessed. Maybe they were trying to warn us. My mother got us to run inside the house. She had to tie the two dogs up at the back of the house. I can remember how they would not stop barking all night long.

That night, the barking had finally stopped. Our two dogs had their throats slit. Looking back, I can't help but think that if our dogs were still around, they might have protected my family from the killer. This elusive fragment of my memory was slowly piecing itself back together.

Doctor Addison

Thursday 19th February 2015

Morning

I caught the 7:34am train to Waterloo station. I was running late. I wanted to do my makeup on the train but I had barely enough space to stand. I'll do it when I get to work. The train was rammed and I could feel a sweaty, hairy, smelly Libyan man pressed up against me. I recognised his accent. I could not understand how the world did nothing to stop these savages from engaging in modern slavery. I skipped breakfast again. I was hungry and needed coffee. I am going to ask Sophie to grab me a bagel as soon as I get to the office. I would get it myself but the queues are too long at this time.

The train stopped at Vauxhall station. I fought someone off for a seat. I heard an announcement. The train had to halt because of signalling errors. Five minutes had passed and the train hadn't moved an inch. I was going to be late again.

Amar phoned me in the afternoon later that day. The first meeting went as expected. The Detective said that he would call back in the evening to make arrangements.

Amar decided to kill a bit of time. He began to read through his grandmother's letter. He remembered that he needed to scatter her ashes. He wished that he had someone to go with him. I wanted to go with him.

Amar's phone rang. The Detective was ready to meet him. They found a quiet place in town. Amar ordered a glass of water and Detective Le Clezio ordered a glass of Cognac.

Detective Le Clezio had figured out who Amar was. He knew that he was from London and that he came here to solve the case of his family's death.

Amar was confounded and impressed.

Detective Le Clezio wrote his fees down on a piece of paper. He said that the figure did not include his expenses.

'No way,' said Amar. 'I will find someone else.'

'I'll tell you what,' said the Detective. 'I can do it for half the price.'

'I can pay you a quarter now and if you solve this case, I will give you all of the money and a bonus,' said Amar.

'We have a deal,' he replied.

He shook his hand.

I will call you tomorrow,' said Detective Le Clezio.

Amar left.

He believed in his heart that he had found the right man.

He went for a walk at the waterfront and called me. He liked being there. He watched the reflection of the light on the water. Hiring the Detective had been our best idea so far.

'What's the weather like?' I asked.

'It's nice,' he said.

I was waiting eagerly for Amar to ask me to join him in Mauritius but he hadn't broached the subject. I really needed some excitement in my life and I was beginning to trust him. I think that if he had asked me then, I would have probably said yes. I wanted to go with him to scatter the ashes of his grandmother. This case had completely taken over my life. It was all I thought about and it was all that I wrote about.

Sometimes Amar calls me late at night. I actually prefer it. I'm a night owl. I'm usually up anyway reading.

I really like Amar's taste in books. We were both huge fans of Orwell and Hemingway and we both thought that Fitzgerald was overrated. He hated Gatsby and so did I. He said that my voice was warm and comforting.

He said that after he returned back to London that we should go out for a drink to celebrate. He asked it so casually like it meant nothing.

I told him that I would love to. He started asking me about my engagement. I told him that I was not really engaged and that I made the whole thing up so we can focus on helping him. He never got around to asking me if I wanted to fly out to Mauritius. I wanted to help him investigate. We kept on talking.

'I think that I am ready,' he said.

'Ready for what?' I asked.

'To scatter my grandmother's ashes,' he said. 'In her letter, she wanted me to scatter them at three places located on the island. The Chamarel Falls, Troux aux Cerfs and Grand Bassin. I will do it tomorrow.'

'I wish that I could be there with you. Call me if you feel lonely. I will be with you on the phone if you need me,' I said.

'Thank you,' said Amar.

I could not stop thinking about the Detective. I wondered what he would uncover about the case. I kept falling in and out of sleep.

I kept on writing until I was too sleepy and then I quietly slipped into bed. I overheard the couple arguing in the flat next to mine. They were arguing about bills. I opened my window and lit a cigarette. I had an emergency pack hidden behind a bookshelf. I was hiding it from myself. I stared up at the sky. There was almost a full moon.

I got up at around 5am and the day stretched out over me, not a minute of it filled. I opened my eyes and listened to the rain against the window.

Amar

Friday 20th February 2015

Morning

Detective Le Clezio phoned me and said that he had
uncovered some interesting information regarding the case.

'When would you be ready to present it to me?' I asked.

'Soon,' he replied. 'I want to capture the footage of the
crime scene first.'

'When are you planning on going?' I asked.

'Probably, later on today,' he said. 'Do you want to come
with me?' he asked.

'Not today,' I said. 'There is something very important
that I need to do.'

'I understand,' he said. 'I just thought I should ask.'

'That's fine,' I said.

I hung up the phone and got into my car which I had
rented for a few days. In my grandmother's letter, she
wanted me to scatter her ashes at Chamarel Falls, Troux
aux Cerfs and Grand Bassin. It was her dying wish. I drove
to Chamarel Falls. The drive took a little over an hour.

It was a warm, windy day and the sky was cloudless. I
should have paid for a taxi but the thrill of the open road
excited me. The Chamarel waterfall streams from the River
du Cap. The water falls along a vertical cliff. The spray
rises to half the height of the waterfall. The footpath was
stiff and slippery. The waterfall was surrounded by lush
vegetation of the Black River Gorges.

I picked up a pamphlet from my hotel lobby that stated that you can watch the waterfall from the upper deck situated at the Chamarel Seven Colored Earth reserve or you can head down the trail to enjoy shallow water swimming.

I stood there watching the water falling and bouncing off the rocks at the bottom. The water from the summit flowed calmly and then dropped aggressively. I looked in detail staring at the colors. I noticed the different shades of grey and when the water turned white. The smell from the spray was a musty odour emanating from the surrounding trees and rocks. I could taste the slight salinity of the freshwater. I closed my eyes and thought about swimming or standing under the falling water.

I trudged down to the bottom of the hill. It was very steep. I finally arrived at the base. The water was directly falling in front of me. I stopped for a moment. I opened the lidded urn. I scattered some of the ashes against the waterfall. The river would pick it up and carry it to the sea. My grandmother loved this place.

I called Doctor Addison.

She asked me how I was feeling.

'I miss my grandmother,' I said. 'I wish that she was still alive. She must have missed this place. We had lived in London for over 25 years. We never returned back here. She planned on visiting but she was scared. She didn't want me to grow up all alone.'

'I'm sure that your grandmother is smiling down on you from heaven,' replied Doctor Addison.

'Thanks,' I said. 'I have finished what I came here to do. I'll call you later on when I get back to Port Louis.'

I hung up the phone. I wanted to call Detective Le Clezio to see how he was getting on. He said that he would call me when he was ready. I decided to drive back to the hotel.

I followed the trail back to my car. I heard a ruffling sound from behind me. Somebody was watching me. I could feel their eyes on me. I was scared.

I ran back to my car. I sped off and noticed a car in my rear view mirror following me. It was either a taxi or a police car. I wasn't sure. Somebody was following me. I wanted to draw them out. I had a golf club that I could use as a weapon.

I noticed the same car again in my rear view mirror. It was a police car. I scribbled the registration plates down on a piece of paper. The road was too quiet. I wanted to stop somewhere crowded. Then I would get out and see who this police officer was. I tried to catch a glimpse of the person in my mirror.

I followed the road into Port Louis. I looked behind me and the car was gone. I waited hoping to see it again but it had vanished. My mind was racing.

I arrived at the lobby of the hotel. I was tired and wanted to rest. I ordered room service. I wanted a cigarette but I had just one left. I went downstairs into the lobby and bought a pack from the machine in the corridor. I went back to my room and turned on the television. There was a strange documentary about the inhabitants of Diego Garcia. These people had been through a lot and were displaced from their island with no monetary compensation or remuneration.

I thought about Doctor Addison. I wanted to call her. I really liked hearing her voice. It soothed and settled me. She asked me how my day went. I said that it was great and I explained how I thought that somebody was following me.

'Are you sure?' She asked. 'Did you see what the person looked like?'

'No but I wrote the registration plates down on a piece of paper,' I replied. 'Shit. I think that it slipped out of my pocket. I can't find it anywhere.'

Doctor Addison asked me about Detective Le Clezio.

I said that I will probably call him tomorrow morning to see how he got on.

I wondered what he would uncover. I sat at my desk and read a book.

Doctor Addison

Saturday 21st February 2015

Morning

Two trains were cancelled this morning which meant that I
arrived at work late. I hated working on saturdays. Luckily
Sophie was on time to make sure that everything was
alright.

I had finished seeing a patient and it was around midday.
I sent Amar a text this morning and asked him to call me.
That was a few hours ago.

I was hungry and had not eaten and so I walked back to
Waterloo station and bought a sandwich. I decided to call
Amar again. His mobile phone was switched off. I sent him
a message to ask if he was okay. Maybe his battery died or
he could have lost his phone. I'm sure that it was nothing.

I checked my call log. The last time I called him was at
11:30 pm which meant that it was 7:30 pm in Mauritius.
What if he went out last night? He was a little tipsy when I
spoke to him. Maybe he went out and got drunk. Could the
killer have tracked him down? He mentioned that
somebody had been following him. Somebody in a police
car.

I should have taken him more seriously. I felt responsible.
Amar went to Chamarel Falls all alone yesterday morning
but had returned back to his hotel. Nobody knew that he
was there. How long do you have to wait before reporting
somebody missing? Please God let Amar be alright.

I had an appointment with a patient but I couldn't think straight. The tip of my fingertips were shaking. I closed my eyes and saw an image of Amar's body floating in a river. It suddenly hit me. He was staying at the Grand hotel in Port Louis. I went on the internet and found a phone number. I dialled it immediately.

'Grand Hotel,' a voice said.

'Tu parle anglais?' I asked.

'Yes. I speak english,' said the receptionist.

'I am looking for my friend. He is staying at your hotel. His name is Amar. He checked in a few days ago. He was supposed to call me this morning but I haven't heard from him. I am worried and I think that he has gone missing. I'm sure that it's nothing. Is he in his room?' I asked.

'He is not in his room,' replied the receptionist.

'Where is he?' I asked.

'The police came looking for him this morning,' she said. 'They took him away.'

'What did they want with him?' I asked.

'They didn't say,' she said.

'That's okay,' I said. 'If you see him. Can you please tell him to call Kate.'

'I will pass the message,' she said.

I said thanks and hung up the phone.

Why had the police taken Amar in? He mentioned that a police car was following him yesterday when he went to Chamarel falls. I was just glad that he was alive.

I tried to call Amar but his phone went to answerphone.

I received a call from a restricted number. I answered it.

'Hello this is Inspector Singh. I am from the Port Louis precinct. Is this a good time to speak?' he asked.

'Yes,' I replied.

'We have somebody in our custody named Amar Biswas,' he said. 'Can you verify his whereabouts yesterday night in the evening? He mentioned that he was on the phone to you.'

'You have to be a little more specific?' I said.

'At around 5pm in Port Louis,' he replied. 'That would make it around 9pm in London.'

'Let me check my call log,' I said. 'Amar was on the phone with me. He was at his hotel.'

'Thank you,' said Inspector Singh.

'What is this in relation to?' I asked.

'I am not at liberty to divulge that information,' he said. 'Thank you Doctor Addison for assisting us. I will be in touch.'

'What about Amar?' I asked. 'Can I speak to him? Is he alright?'

'We are going to release him shortly,' he said. 'You can speak to him after.'

'Thank you,' I said.

Amar called me after a couple of hours.

'Amar what happened?' I asked. 'Are you okay?'

'I am fine,' he said, 'It's Detective Le Clezio.'

'Is he alright?'

'No,' replied Amar. 'He was found dead in his car outside the crime scene in Montagne Blanche.'

'Oh no,' I said. 'What happened?'

'The police took me in for questioning. They suspected me at first but luckily my alibi checked out. They had me on CCTV buying cigarettes in the hotel lobby at the time of the murder. Lividity placed the time of death at around 5pm. I was at the hotel at that time,' explained Amar.

'What else did they say?' I asked.

'I had to come clean about everything,' said Amar. 'I told them why I was here and why I hired the Detective. I told them who I was and what happened to my family all those years ago.'

'Amar I think you should come back to London,' I said. 'It's not safe out there. Get on the next flight.'

'That won't be possible,' replied Amar. 'The police seized my passport. I won't be allowed to leave the country until they close Detective Le Clezio's murder investigation.'

'That's terrible,' I said.

'At least we know that the killer is still out there,' said Amar.

'That's right,' I said. 'Amar you mentioned somebody following you yesterday.'

'Yes,' he said. 'It was somebody in a police car. I should have mentioned that to Inspector Singh. I wrote the license plate on a piece of paper but I can't find it anywhere.'

'What are you going to do?' I asked.

'I'm going to stay at the hotel,' he said. 'Hang around the lobby in front of the cameras where it's safe.'

'Good idea,' I said. 'Amar call me if you need anything okay.'

'Thank you,' said Amar.

He hung up the phone.

I was speechless. Who could have done this? It was late in the afternoon and I had not eaten. I was too shocked to eat.

I called Amar back to say that we needed to find Detective Le Clezio's camera. I thought that there may be a clue on who the killer is.

'I have already mentioned it to the police. They searched his entire vehicle but his phone or camera could not be retrieved,' said Amar. 'I suggested that it might be somewhere inside the house. Inspector Singh said that it was far too dangerous and that he was not sending anyone inside. He said that the roof of the house could collapse at any moment. I still want to find it.'

Amar's case fascinated me but I quickly realised that it was more dangerous than I had previously thought. Someone was killed. I feared for Amar's safety. I tried to arrange time off work. I wanted to be there by his side.

Doctor Addison

Sunday 22nd February 2015

Morning

'How are you feeling?' I said to Amar over the phone.

'I woke up feeling restless,' he said. 'I feel like a drooping flag on a windless day. I am going to scatter my grandmother's ashes at Troux Aux Cerfs later today.'

'Amar. It's too dangerous,' I said,

'I need to draw out whoever was following me,' he said. 'I need to get the license plate. I wished that I hadn't lost the note.'

'Be careful Amar,' I said. 'Stay on the phone with me and keep me updated on everything.'

Amar drove through Curepipe and in the direction of Troux Aux Cerfs. He was going there to scatter the ashes of his dead grandmother. It was her dying wish. She wrote it in her letter.

Amar stared listlessly through the windshield at the sky. He gazed at the pure white cloud edges, distinct yet so sharply etched you could write on it. He noticed a bird etching a slow circle in the sky.

The Troux aux Cerfs crater had been extinct for a long time and the crater floor was heavily wooded. A tarred road lead gently up to and around the rim. There were benches for rest and reflection.

Amar felt that it could rain at any minute. He got out of his car and walked around the perimeter road. There was a great view of the surrounding area. The view was breathtaking. Amar said that he wouldn't recommend trying to climb down to the crater. The rough path looked unsafe. The crater was lined with trees and a green covered base.

Amar had me on the phone. He breathed the crisp clean air. He felt like somebody was following him. He could feel another presence like he was being watched. The sky darkened. He wanted to get closer to the crater. There were crunchy leaves underneath his feet. Mauritius didn't have spring or Autumn. Just summer and winter.

Everything looked monotonous as he stared at the water at the bottom of the crater. He stroked a hollowed out branch with his fingertips. The hollow sound reverberated through him. He stared down at the forest glade. The hill rose steadily, each one higher than the last.

He stared down below. He was very high up and felt as though vertigo had taken hold of him. Everything around him froze. He felt dizzy. All his strength was drained. He felt immobilized and then collapsed against a post. He gasped for air. He was barely able to support his body. Amar thought about jumping but he would never do it. He scattered the ashes and thought about his grandmother.

Amar spotted a blurry figure from a distance walking towards him and growing clearer. A tall beautiful woman appeared before him. Was he dreaming?

'Have you been following me?' asked Amar.

'Amar are you okay?' I yelled over the telephone.

Amar lowered the phone but did not hang up.

I moved the phone closer to my ear.

'Just keeping an eye on you and making sure you don't do anything stupid,' she said. 'My chief's orders. Why are you here?'

'I came here to scatter my grandmother's ashes. It was her dying wish,' Amar said.

'I hope that you are not planning on jumping,' she said.

'I just want to be with my family,' he said.

'I know how that feels,' she said. She reached out her hand and placed it on his.

'What's your name?' asked Amar.

'Detective Maya Kohli,' she said. She handed her police I.D over to Amar.

'I am a homicide detective,' she said.

'Can I get a lift to my car?' she asked.

'Sure,' replied Amar. 'Where did you park?'

'Further down the road,' she pointed.

They went inside Amar's car for shelter from the falling rain. I imagined the rain coming down in sheets. He was lost in thought as he looked out of the window. Maya glanced at Amar and he felt breathless. He couldn't stop staring at her hair. She had gorgeous eyes and smelled like cherries. Amar wanted to say something.

'You should not be here,' Amar said.

'What do you mean?' she asked.   police detectives

'Smart beautiful women become lawyers not cops,' said Amar.

Maya tried not to smile.

'Where are you parked?' he asked.

'Further up,' she said. 'I read your case file this morning. I am sorry that your family is not with you. I know what that is like.'

'I am just trying to move on,' he said. 'But it's hard.'

'I heard that you were looking for Detective Le Clezio's camera,' asked Maya. 'Do you know where it could be?'

'I am certain that it is somewhere inside the house. It has to be,' said Amar.

'Should we go and see if we can find it?' Maya said.

He paused and said nothing.

'You are not scared are you?' asked Maya.

'No,' replied Amar. 'We are not allowed to trespass on the crime scene.'

'It's not trespassing if you are with me. I'm a homicide detective,' she said. 'It's my job to investigate.'

'How long have you been following me since?' asked Amar.

'Only since this morning?' she said.

'But I saw you the other day on my way back from Chamarel Falls,' said Amar.

'I didn't think that you saw me,' she replied. 'We have been keeping an eye on you for some time now. We thought that we could draw out the person who killed your family. I was keeping an eye on you in case somebody tried anything.'

'I don't believe you,' said Amar.

'I am here to make sure that you are safe,' said Maya.

'I'm not buying it,' said Amar. 'How did you know that I was here in Mauritius?'

'Your passport flagged up on the system,' she said. 'Look if I wanted to kill you I can do it right now.' She pulled out her gun. 'Or yesterday when you were at Chamarel falls. You were all alone by the waterfall. I could have shot you from long range and threw your body into the river. I'm not trying to scare you. I want to help you Amar.'

I sent Amar a text. I said that he should be careful and that he should leave me on the call in case she tries anything. She could be our suspect.

'Who is that?' asked Maya.

'It's just my Doctor,' he said.

Amar put the phone to his ears.

'I don't think that we can trust her,' I whispered.

'What do you mean?' asked Amar.

'Just be careful,' I said.

'Don't worry,' replied Amar. 'I am going with her to the abandoned house to see if we can locate Detective Le Clezio's camera phone.'

'Are you sure about her?' I asked.

'Yes, why shouldn't I be? Don't worry I checked her identification. She is with the police,' said Amar.

I sighed.

'I will call you back,' he said.

Amar pretended to hang up. I decided to record the phone call.

'You have a Doctor?' asked Maya.

'Why does that surprise you?' asked Amar.

'It doesn't,' she said. 'My car's here. Jump in.'

Amar got inside Maya's police car. The drive didn't take long. She sped through the traffic.

Amar pressed his face against the glass and stared at the scenery. His face protruded like a bubble pressed against glass.

'What about my car?' asked Amar.

'We can pick it up later,' Maya replied.

Amar's mind was racing. He felt determined. Blood was pumping hard into his arms and legs. He felt fearless.

They arrived at the town. Amar finally grasped what he had gotten himself into. He was not thinking straight. The closer he got, the more his fear grew. The silence was suddenly drowned out by the sound of loud caws. He followed the sound to a crow perched on a branch. Amar was not ready and his hands were shaking. He sipped some whisky from his flask and was preparing to step out of the vehicle.

'Give me some,' asked Maya.

Amar passed the flask over to her and she finished off what was left.

'There is probably a clue on the camera phone,' suggested Maya. 'We have to find it.'

What if Maya is the killer? I got the feeling that Amar was trying to prove to us that he was not scared.

'Hold on a second,' said Amar. 'I just need to make a quick call.'

Amar pretended to call me even though I was listening in the whole time.

He explained the situation to me. He sent me a text message discreetly to call Inspector Singh and to ask him about Maya. He sent over her badge number.

'I am really sorry but I don't think that I can go with you,' voiced Amar.

Amar

Sunday 22nd February 2015

Evening

'Why don't you wait outside the house and I'll go in and look,' proposed Maya. 'Don't worry you can stay on the phone with your girlfriend if you get scared.'

I didn't reply. She was clearly baiting me. I followed closely behind her and I was starting to get lost. I couldn't stop staring at her. She was too beautiful to be a police detective. I could easily imagine her as an actress in a shampoo commercial.

'Why are you really here?' she asked me.

'I am here to find whoever killed my family. They didn't deserve to die. I am here for justice,' I said.

'Do you have any leads or suspects?' asked Maya.

'Not yet,' I replied. 'Why do you want to help me?'

'It's my job and I want to solve this case,' she said. 'I read the case report from the night of the 5th. I'm sorry for your loss.'

'Is there any chance I can get a look at the case report?' I said.

'I will see what I can do,' replied Maya.

'Please try,' I said. 'I think that there is something that I am not quite remembering.'

'What is it?' asked Maya.

'I'm not sure,' I said. 'Thank you for helping me.'
She smiled.

The walk was creepy. There was something about Maya that had dispelled my fear. There was only a few hours of light left. The entrance was blocked off by cones and red tape. She parked the car and we walked over the tape. There was a hesitance in both me and her. I tried to remember how it was all those years ago. So much had changed and the road leading up to the house was a shorter distance. In my mind the walk seemed longer. It was probably because I was only five and my legs were much shorter. The area was covered with wild grass and vines. The house looked dilapidated. I walked past a pond. The water was green. There were small logs floating in it. The logs were smooth and turning imperceptibly. The water was shivering and had gone white in places under the light. There were shrines and golden statues of Hindu Gods and deities that had been stolen. The dark trees swayed and whispered. My mind drifted and I got a flashback of the night of the murder. I got flashes of me running out of the house and to the neighbour's house. I imagined somebody chasing after me getting closer and closer. Almost instantly, I felt exactly how I felt on the night of the 5th. I wanted to turn back. Maya could sense that I was scared.

'I don't think that I can do this,' I said. 'I don't want you to go inside. I don't think I can stay here any longer.'

Maya walked over to me,

'Why don't you come inside the house with me? It's not that bad. Come on. I'll let you hold on to my gun,' she said.

She held open my palm and thrust a gun into my hand.

I did not know how to respond. I was stuck between a simultaneous state of arousal and fear. There was something about Maya and her soft voice. She was very good at convincing me but I got the feeling that she wanted to keep me nearby. I just wanted to fling her against the side of her car and kiss her. I took her gun and said that I would wait for her by the car.

'What about you?' I asked.

'I've got another gun on me. Don't worry about me. Just stay vigilant,' she said.

Maya crept into the abandoned house. I could tell that she felt sorry for me. After all, this was the place where I lost my whole family.

I called Doctor Addison.

'What happened?' she said.

'The front entrance is blocked off. Maya has gone into the house through the rear entrance. I told her to look near to where the Detective had died,' I said to Doctor Addison over the telephone.

I stayed sharp and focused in case somebody snuck up on me. My heart was hammering. The sun had set and it was starting to get dark.

I asked Doctor Addison how long had passed.

She said that she should have been out by now.

Why was she taking so long? I thought to myself.

'Maybe you can try phoning her,' suggested Doctor Addison.

'I don't have her number,' I replied. 'Should I go in and see if she is alright?'

'No,' she replied. 'That's what she wants you to do. I think that she is trying to lure you into the house to kill you. Amar turn around right now.'

'I'm going in,' I said.

Doctor Addison pleaded with me but my mind was already made up.

'Stay on the phone,' I said. 'If she tries anything you will hear everything.'

Doctor Addison reluctantly agreed. My heart was hammering. I'm going to get in closer. I charged inside.

The phone reception cut off for a few seconds and then reconnected. I crept slowly into the house. The walls had cracked concrete and bits of dust fell on me. I felt chilly. I bet the killer was here. He could be watching us. The patient watcher waiting to strike. I walked through the arches and around the rear entrance. It was particularly eerie. I had come to a small desolate area and I stopped walking. I trudged into one of the dark rooms. This place gave me the creeps. There was visual evidence that my family lived here a long time ago. This was the house of horror. I prowled around. I figured that I didn't have a lot of time. I called Maya's name out loud and I got no response. This house was my obsession. This was where evil lurked. I searched for something, anything, clues but my mind was elsewhere. I just wanted to get out. I walked on top of a rotting plank. I lost my balance and leaned against the wall and dust fell from the ceiling. Something was peering at me, watching me from afar. I was sure of it. I arrived at the arch of the house and called her name.

'Maya. Are you okay? Should I call for help?' I bellowed.

I got no answer. I walked past the garage which was covered by a tin roof. Just at that moment, I remembered when I woke up at exactly two minutes past midnight all those years ago. In my mind, I could remember the sound of the rain hitting the tin roof. I prayed for it not to rain.

I approached the living room door and nudged it open. The door squealed on its hinges as I entered the eerie and neglected room. Inside it reeked of beech mast. I felt like I was breathing through a mask. It was dark and the windows let in very little light. I put Doctor Addison on loudspeaker and switched on the torch light from my phone. The light wasn't very strong. I pointed it around hoping to catch a glimpse of Maya. I checked to see if the roof was stable. I walked further into the house and approached a light switch. I flicked it on but it was not working. I noticed more red tape. I heard a ruffling sound in the distance. I called Maya's name again but heard nothing back. I pointed the phone's torch up. The roof had a big hole and I could see right upstairs. I decided to walk around. The weight of my feet split the planks on the floor.

My heart was pounding. I was not sure what I was afraid of. I looked around. My hands were trembling. I bumped my knee against something. I was walking quietly into another foyer.

'Amar. Are you okay?' asked Doctor Addison.

'I want to lie down but I want to leave here first. If I don't lie down. I'm going to pass out,' I said over the telephone.

Doctor Addison asked me to breath. Suddenly I heard a voice.

'Over here,' said a voice.

My heart started hammering.

It was Maya.

'Why didn't you reply?' I asked.

'I didn't hear you,' said Maya.

'The house is empty,' she remarked. 'There's nobody here.'

'Did you find the camera?' I asked.

'Yes,' she said. 'I cleared the rubble and dug it out. I tried to switch it on but the battery is dead. I am certain that this belonged to the Detective.'

I wanted to leave the house as soon as possible. I grabbed Maya's hand and had a final glance before we left through a side exit. Outside, the sun had fully set and there were no lights apart from my phone's torch. I followed the pool of blood to Detective Le Clezio's vehicle which was still parked and covered with red tape. There were no trespassing signs everywhere. I wanted to peer inside but I was too scared to look.

Doctor Addison was still on the phone. I explained that Maya had found Detective Le Clezio's camera phone in the rubble.

'Maybe there is something on the memory card that the Detective was alluding to,' I said.

I told her that I wanted to go back to my hotel and check out the information from Detective Le Clezio's camera.

'I will come with you,' a voice said. It was Maya.

My battery was running low.

'I'll call you back in a bit,' I said. I hung up the phone.

Doctor Addison sent me a message. I didn't read it. I switched my phone to airplane mode to preserve battery life.

I got into Maya's police car and we drove off. I felt at ease being around her.

'Wait! What should I do about my car?' I said.

'It's parked close to Troux aux Cerfs,' replied Maya. 'Do you really want to go there this late?'

'You are right but I left my grandmother's ashes in there. I hope that the car doesn't get stolen,' I said.

'This isn't London. Car thefts are very rare here. Anyway it's a rental,' she said. 'Look I'll drop you off at your hotel and we can go together in the morning to pick up your car.'

'Okay,' I said.

'Where are you staying?' asked Maya.

'The Grand Hotel in Port Louis,' I said.

'I need to get changed quickly. Do you mind if we stop over at my place quickly before we head to yours? I live only 10 minutes from Port Louis,' she said.

'Sure,' I replied.

I felt tired. I wondered whether Maya was taking me somewhere to kill me. I didn't care at that point. The car started to slow down. I had no idea where we were. She parked her car and we took the elevator up to her apartment.

I switched my phone off airplane mode. There were several messages and missed calls from Doctor Addison.

'My friend wants to know where I am. What should I say?' I said.

'Is that your girlfriend?' asked Maya.

'I'll just say we are at Castle Rock apartments heading into flat 32.'

'You don't trust me, do you?' suggested Maya.

'Do you blame me?' I replied.

'I guess not,' she said.

I walked into her apartment and went out to the balcony.

'Do you mind if I smoke?' I said.

'Go ahead,' Maya said. 'There's an ashtray by the window. I'll be ready in a few minutes. Then we can head over to your place.'

Maya's apartment was sparsely decorated as if no one lived here. The art on the wall was modern and vaguely depressing. She had lots of books on criminology and the study of forensic evidence. I stared down a dark corridor and noticed a piano in the corner of the room. There was a sheet music for Chopin Nocturne op.9 No.2.

I asked her where the camera phone was and she said that she had left it in her car.

I got a message from Doctor Addison which read don't trust Maya. Remember what your grandmother wrote to you in her letter. She was right. I needed to get out of here while there was still time.

'Can I grab your car keys? I'm just going to grab the camera from your car. I want to see what's on it,' I said.

'Just hold on. I am almost ready,' she said. 'Check the cabinet next to the fridge. I think there is some scotch left over. Just help yourself.'

Amar

Monday 23rd February 2015

Morning

I woke up back in my bed at the Grand hotel. I switched on
my phone. It was fully charged. My phone beeped. There
was a message on it, sent several hours ago. There was
over 24 missed calls from Doctor Addison. What did I do
last night? Why was Doctor Addison phoning me so many
times? I pulled the duvet over my head.

I tried desperately to make sense of an elusive fragment
of my memory. I can almost hear her words, but it shifts
from me again. I can't get a handle on it.

My head was spinning. I got out of bed and went to the
toilet to piss. I returned back to bed and saw Maya lying
there naked. It all started coming back to me.

Last night, Maya and I reviewed the video footage from
the memory card and we finished off two bottles of scotch.
Next thing I remembered how she climbed on top of me
and started kissing me. It's all a blur.

I didn't want to wake her up. I started looking through all
the unread messages from Doctor Addison. The messages
were about Maya and how I should not trust her.
Something about her badge number. Doctor Addison's
message stated that she had confirmation from Inspector
Singh that Maya was never assigned to this case. I checked
the time. It was 10am which meant that it was 2pm in
London.

I got dressed and walked to the hotel lobby. I phoned Doctor Addison. I got no response. I was storming up and down the lobby waiting for her to call me back.

My phone rang. It was her. She was with a patient. She must have gone back to work this morning.

'What happened last night?' asked Doctor Addison.

'I don't remember much,' I replied. 'I think I may have had an alcohol induced blackout.'

'Did Maya drug you?' she asked.

'I don't think that she drugged me,' I replied.

'What happened?' she asked.

'I woke up and Maya was fast asleep in my bed?' I said.

'Did you sleep with her?' asked Doctor Addison.

I did not reply.

'Amar, I made it perfectly clear what I thought about trusting Maya. Did you read any of my messages?' asked Doctor Addison. 'Have you forgotten what your grandmother wrote to you in her letter about trusting complete strangers?'

I tried to come up with a lie.

'I had a lot to drink and I only saw the messages this morning,' I replied.

'Was that before or after you slept with her?' asked Doctor Addison.

I couldn't answer her.

'What did Inspector Singh say about her?' I asked.

'Inspector Singh confirmed that Maya is a homicide Detective. He also confirmed that she has not officially been assigned to this case. She is working rogue. I bet you that she is connected to your family's killer. She is probably working for them,' claimed Doctor Addison.

'She is upstairs now,' I said. 'What should I do?'

'I don't think that we can trust her,' said Doctor Addison. 'What do we really know about her? I have a gut feeling that she is probably connected to whoever killed your family.'

'I don't think so,' I said. 'She found the camera. I don't feel afraid of anything when I am with her.'

Doctor Addison said that I was just blinded because I slept with her and that I should think with my head.

'She probably killed Detective Le Clezio,' suggested Doctor Addison.

'Please Kate,' I pleaded. 'I need you here with me. If there are 2 of us we can solve this case much quicker. You are the only person that I can trust.'

'I am making arrangements,' replied Doctor Addison. 'I am here on the phone if you need me.'

'Maya is upstairs,' I said. 'What should I do?'

'Let's wait and see if she comes downstairs,' suggested Doctor Addison.

I waited in the lobby and after an hour had passed, I decided to go up. I called Doctor Addison and I left her on the phone so she could hear everything in case Maya tried to kill me.

I stayed vigilant and headed back to my room. I unlocked the door and walked in.

'Maya, are you still here?' I got no reply.

I leaned over the bed but she was gone. Her shoes and clothes were all gone. I walked into the bathroom and checked to see if I could find her. I saw a sticky note on my bathroom mirror. It had Maya's name written on it with her phone number.

'Amar. Is everything alright?' asked Doctor Addison.

'She is gone,' I replied.

'Did you find anything useful on the Detective's camera phone?' asked Doctor Addison.

'Not yet,' I said.

I walked over to my laptop and the memory card from the camera phone was gone. Maya had stolen it.

I asked Doctor Addison if I should phone her and ask for it back.

'That's what she wants you to do, she said. 'I don't think that you should do that. Try and remember? Did you get a look at any of the files?' asked Doctor Addison.

'Barely,' I replied.

'I am certain that she is connected to your family's killer,' said Doctor Addison. 'We cannot trust her. Why else would she take the memory card?'

'You are right,' I said.

My phone rang. It was Maya. I answered.

'Where is the memory card from the camera?' I asked.

'I waited for you and after you had not returned back, I decided to go home,' she said. 'I took it because I wanted to have a copy. Don't freak out, I copied and pasted all the files onto your laptop.'

I switched on my laptop.

'It's all saved on a folder named Le Clezio's memory card,' said Maya.

'Thanks,' I said.

Maya proposed that we meet up in the evening.

I agreed and hung up the telephone. I really liked her but something held me back.

I phoned Doctor Addison back immediately and explained everything.

'She may have tampered with the case files and documents,' said Doctor Addison.

'I'm confused. Please I need you here,' I pleaded. 'I really need your help. You are the only one that I can trust.'

'Amar I can't just leave work. Do not worry. I am here on the phone if you need me,' said Doctor Addison.

I explained how Maya and I had agreed to meet up later this evening.

'You cannot meet her,' she said. 'You need to move to another hotel right away. You are in danger. She could be an assassin.'

'You are right,' I said.

'Pack your bags but don't check out. Go to another hotel and check in and stay there and don't tell anyone that you are staying there or that you have moved hotel,' said Doctor Addison.

'What do I do if she calls and arranges to meet up this evening?' I asked.

'You should meet her in the lobby of the Grand hotel. Whatever you do, do not invite her upstairs. You need to be out in public at all times. I am going to hire another Private Detective to investigate her,' said Doctor Addison.

I agreed. I hung up the phone and packed my bags. I got into a taxi and checked in at another hotel. The hotel was located on the outskirts of Port Louis. I unpacked my bags and had a shower. I drank way too much last night. I looked out at the unbroken view of the town and the sea from my room window.

I watched the videos from Detective Le Clezio's camera phone before his untimely demise. It was very creepy and the picture quality was not great. I could not recognise anything from when I was 5.

The video panned into one of the rooms. I noticed a porcelain doll in my room next to the closet where I had been hiding. That doll belonged to Neha. She use to carry that doll everywhere with her. There was something about the doll's eyes that reminded me of something but I couldn't quite put my finger on it. I remember dreaming about a little girl that followed me and she was holding onto that doll. Maybe it's Neha. It was a similar doll but the little girl was not my sister. It was somebody else.

Detective Le Clezio's hand was shaking and then he dropped the camera. It's not clear but it looked like there was somebody else in the house with him. You can hear him in the video running out of the house. Someone was chasing after him all the way to his car and then the video cuts off.

If I hand this over to the police, I will get charged for trespassing onto the crime scene. The video footage was not clear and did not confirm anything. Maybe Maya had tampered with it. I decided to keep it. I hailed a taxi to Troux Aux Cerfs to pick up my rental car. My grandmother's ashes was still in the glove compartment. I had just one place left. I decided to go on another day. I went back to my hotel to rest.

Doctor Addison

Monday 23rd February 2015

Evening

I was worried sick. All Amar had to do was call me to let me know that he was okay. I thought that he was dead. I thought that Maya had killed him.

I'm not even upset that he slept with Maya last night. I am happy for him. I just wished that he was a little more careful. We don't know anything about this woman. It felt like a trap.

I rang him yesterday after I spoke to Inspector Singh and the idiot switched off his phone so I wouldn't interrupt his lovemaking. I was trying to warn him.

Then he calls me at around 2pm which meant that it was 10am in Mauritius to say that he was alive. I don't think that I am overreacting. I actually thought that he was dead.

That's all in the past now and we both agreed that we had to focus on the present. I got another call from Amar. Maya rang him and said that she needed to explain something important to him. I told him to say that he would call her back later and that he was busy.

Amar was at a bar waiting for the new Private Investigator. His name was Mr Shen. I personally hired him to see if he could dig up any information on Maya and Dev. We needed to know whether they could be trusted. I had a feeling that they might be connected to the killer.

Amar rang me and brought me up to speed.

I asked him how his meeting with Detective Shen went and he said that it was as expected. I had a hunch that Maya was probably an assassin. I didn't trust her. Inspector Singh confirmed that Maya was a homicide Detective but we couldn't understand why she was hellbent on pursuing this case.

I explained to Detective Shen that I was certain that she was connected to Amar's family's murder. The Detective said that he would do his best to uncover the truth.

I told him to find out as much as he could. I wanted him to keep me updated on everything. Me, Amar and Detective Shen were working together on this one.

Amar met Maya at the lobby of the Grand hotel. He asked her what she needed to speak to him about. Amar said it looked as though she wanted to speak but the words had evaporated off her tongue. I reminded Amar that Maya may have tampered with the case documents and that we shouldn't trust her. She probably killed Detective Le Clezio at the house. I wanted to know everything about her. Why had she tracked Amar down? Why was she eager to help him? There was a lot that she was not telling us.

Maya asked if they can go upstairs and take a look at the video again. She reached out her hand and started playing with Amar's hair. He moved her hand away. He was still not sure whether he could trust her and told her to wait. He bought his laptop from his room and they had a look at the videos together in the lobby.

She asked Amar if his girlfriend from the telephone was starting to get jealous. He replied that I was not his girlfriend.

'But you like her?' suggested Maya.

'She is my Doctor. I don't think that I can trust you,' said Amar.

'Why?' asked Maya.

'We spoke to Inspector Singh,' said Amar. 'He confirmed that you are a homicide Detective but he said that this case is not even in your jurisdiction. My grandmother said that I should not trust anybody. I hope that you can understand.'

Maya looked dejected.

'I have a surprise for you,' said Maya.

She handed the police report from the night of the 5th over to Amar.

Amar thanked her.

'Do you trust me now?' she asked.

'Yes,' said Amar.

Amar skimmed through all of the information on the report. He took a picture of the documents and emailed them over to me. I had a skim through.

Amar and Maya watched the video again but he could not remember anything. Amar had an idea. He remembered that his mother kept a photo album upstairs in the study. If Amar had a look at the photographs it may jolt his memory.

'Let's go there and find it,' suggested Maya.

She had a cigarette between her lips. Amar struck a match and lit it.

'You are happy aren't you?' She asked.

'I don't know,' replied Amar. 'At least I am not unhappy.'

'Should we go?' suggested Maya.

'When? Now?' asked Amar. 'I thought that you were joking.'

Amar said that he needed to call me to get some advice. He phoned me and then explained what Maya had proposed. The thought of him being in the house alone with her worried me.

I whispered over the phone and said that Maya was probably planning on luring him to the house to kill him.

Amar whispered back that they had been to the house alone before and that she didn't kill him then.

I did not trust her. I said that he shouldn't go to the house especially this late.

'Fine,' said Maya. 'You better listen to your girlfriend.'

'Wait,' said Amar. 'Where are you going?'

'I am going to see if I can find the photo album,' replied Maya.

I could hear the whole argument over the telephone.

'Let her go,' I said softly over the phone.

She stormed out of the lobby. Amar chased after her in the rain.

'I don't want you to go tonight,' he said. 'Look there is a storm brewing. I will come with you tomorrow during the day.'

'I'll be fine. I'm a police officer. I have a gun on me. I don't think that anybody is going to try anything,' she said.

'I want you to promise me that you will not go tonight,' asked Amar.

Amar had not hung up. I could hear the whole conversation over the telephone. It sounded like Amar was kissing her. Why did he leave me on hold. Was he trying to make me jealous?

I tried to listen in. He was still kissing her. I prayed to God that they don't go back to bed together. I wanted to hang up the phone but I was compelled. I did not want to hear any of this.

Amar walked with her to her car. He kissed her and said goodnight. Then she drove off. I felt relieved.

He grabbed his laptop from the lobby and took a taxi back to his second hotel. Once he arrived, he carefully checked and double checked that all of the doors and windows were locked. Exhausted he finally climbed into bed. He had been praying lately so maybe he did believe in God.

I heard a noise but it was just the wind. I saw a silhouette of a body hovering over me. I got scared and called Amar. Was it just a dream? I told him about the little girl appearing in my dreams holding onto a porcelain doll. Amar said that he had the same dream.

I told him that he did the right thing.

Amar stayed on the phone with me. We talked for hours.

'You did the right thing. We cannot trust Maya until we find out the truth,' I said. 'The Private Detective sent me a message and said that he has found out some interesting information about Maya that is linked to you.'

'What is it?' asked Amar.

'I don't know yet,' I said. 'We will find out tomorrow.'

'I will call him first thing tomorrow morning,' said Amar.

The night had fully settled and the moon hung at the top of the sky.

Amar remarked how Mauritius had a star filled sky unlike London. 'You cannot see anything in London because of the light pollution,' he said.

I forgot to hang up the phone. I could hear Amar breathing. He was fast asleep. I just laid there and listened to him sleep.

Amar

Tuesday 24th February 2015

Morning

I called Detective Shen. I met him at a bar near the waterfront. He said that he had uncovered some interesting information regarding the case.

I sat down and asked him what he had uncovered regarding Maya and Dev. He had a deadoned face as if he hadn't been fed as a baby. His hair was cut longer than the norm. There was a lanky grace in his movement.

'Brace yourself,' he said.

'I'm ready,' I replied.

'I'll start with Dev first,' he said.

'What have you uncovered?' I asked.

'Dev is clean. He is just a taxi driver. I can't find anything that ties him to anything. He has a clean record with no previous misdemeanors or any history of violence,' explained the Private Investigator.

'What about Maya?' I asked.

'Brace yourself,' he said.

He handed me an envelope. The edges of the paper tingled against my fingers. I opened it and peered at the photographs.

He pointed at a picture of my father and a very tall policeman. My father had his arm around him.

'This is Maya's father,' said the Detective.

'They must have been good friends,' I suggested.

The Private Investigator showed me a picture of a couple lying in bed, bludgeoned to death. He pointed at the picture.

'That is Maya's father and her mother,' said the Private Investigator.

I shuddered.

He handed over another set of photographs.

'Put it away,' I gasped. 'That's my family.'

'You need to see this,' pointed the Private Investigator. 'Look at the size of the wounds. They were all murdered in their sleep in a similar fashion to your family. Maya may believe that both yours and her cases are connected. Her parents died one month before your parents. Whoever killed her parents probably killed your parents. A similar blade was used and both murders are almost identical in style.'

Everything had slowed down again. I wanted to leap out of my body. I should have trusted her. Maya was just like me. She had been through exactly what I had been through. We were both the same. We were both looking for the same killer.

I was totally wrong about her. I decided to make amends. I wanted to call her and apologise. I wanted to hold her in my arms and tell her that it was okay. I was glad that I had met her. I guess I'm not alone in this world. We have each other and in some crazy way, that's enough.

I got out my phone and called her. I got no answer. I called her again. I realised now that this was what Maya wanted to explain to me last night. We can start over again. I felt bad because of how cold I was to her yesterday.

I wrote out a text message saying that I was sorry for not trusting her and that I know the truth.

I got a call from Maya. I answered it. She was at the abandoned house and had found my family's photo album from when I was a child.

'I told you not to go there alone. What is that pinging sound?' I asked.

'It's just the rain,' she said. 'The garage roof is made of tin.'

I asked her to send the photos.

She said that she will email them over to me now.

Suddenly, I could hear a very loud gasp. It sounded like she was being strangled.

'Are you okay?' I screamed over the telephone.

The line sounded muffled. I could hear her fighting back until finally she stopped struggling. I could hear somebody else. I wanted the killer to say something and leave me with a clue.

'Maya,' I continued screaming her voice down the end of the telephone. 'Please! Just let her go.'

I was trying to scare the killer with my screams. There was probably nobody for miles. I warned her not to go there alone. I imagined his shadow enveloping over her body and cutting off her air supply.

'Don't please,' I pleaded.

Finally the call disconnected. I got into my car and drove to the abandoned house. I phoned the police and explained everything. They sent out a police squad to the property.

My arms and legs were shaking uncontrollably while I was driving on the highway. I was tired and tried desperately to stay alert. My heart was hammering. I trusted in her ability to take care of herself but looking back, I should have protected her. It's all my fault. My eyes started tearing.

A row of police cruisers were already parked on both sides of the street. I saw my reflection in the rear view mirror. The early morning light from the sun had blinded me and my face looked pale and grim.

I walked on unsure rubbery legs as I got out of my car. I forgot to call Doctor Addison to tell her the terrible news. I was afraid that I was going to break down in front of everyone. Think and focus your thoughts, I said to myself but I couldn't think in straight lines.

By the time I arrived at the house, ambulances were already there. Maya was on a stretcher. The paramedics had placed her inside the ambulance. I watched as they tried to revive her. I was horrified. I was too confused and shocked to scream. My heart was pounding.

The police questioned me. They asked me if I had an alibi. I explained how I was at my hotel the whole time and that the staff could verify it through the CCTV cameras.

I was certain that my alibi would check out.

Just then, we got word that Maya was alive. She was still hanging on. I asked the Police Inspector if it was okay for me to see her. He said yes and we followed the ambulance to the hospital.

'I doubt that we will find anything much here to give us a DNA profile of the suspect,' said one of the policemen.

She was covered in bandages and breathing through a tube.

The Doctor said that it won't take long before she passes away. The merciful blackness came over her but I reached out and grabbed her hand.

'Fight Maya. I know that you can do it,' I cried.

The Doctor said that she needed time alone to recuperate.

I asked the policeman if I was free to go after I gave my statement.

He said that it was fine as long as I didn't try and go back to the abandoned house.

I asked him if anybody else was spotted near the crime scene.

'We are still working on it,' he replied.

I was sure that they had patrol cars in the area. I just wanted Maya to pull through. I should have trusted her. I just want another chance to speak to her and to tell her that I know that we both share the same pain. I was no longer alone. At the same time, I felt a deep loneliness that I had never known before. A sense of perspective transformed. Things far away that I could finally touch. Things blurry that I could see clearly.

Doctor Addison

Night

It was a dark windy night and all this talk of murder had left my heart racing. Was there someone in my flat or had my nightmares drifted into reality. Downstairs, I could hear the return of a long lost sound. I walked barefoot to the edge of the steps and stood there listening, my toes pressed against the plush carpet. I hovered in the doorway, watching. I thought I heard something. There it was again. The slightest creek in the floorboards.

I walked home late the other night. I thought that someone was following me. A creepy little girl holding onto a doll was chasing after me in my dreams last night. I wondered what it meant. Was it Amar's youngest sister trying to tell me something from beyond the grave?

A floorboard creaked on the left side of the bedroom. I heard a tiny sound but it was unmistakable. I held my breath until my chest ached. I sat tensely at the edge of my bed.

Finally I saw a silhouette of a body. A powerful hateful energy. Our eyes met. Even in the darkness her eyes burnt through me. I could not believe that this was happening.

Then I yelled and everything had faded away into the darkness. I decided to sleep with a knife under my pillow. I wanted it to be daytime. The night frightened me and I hated that I lived all alone.

Doctor Addison

Wednesday 25th February 2015

Morning

The following morning Amar called me.

'Where are you?' I asked.

'I'm driving to Grand Bassin,' he said. 'I'm going to scatter the remaining ashes.'

'Keep me on the phone,' I said. 'Amar I have been thinking.'

'Thinking about what?' asked Amar.

'About you, this case and putting it to rest,' I said.

'What are you talking about?' he asked.

'I want to be there with you,' I said. 'I have paid for flights to Mauritius.'

'But it's not safe,' said Amar. 'I don't want you to come. I have changed my mind. I am not here to force my twisted soul into your life. I don't want you to get hurt.'

'Amar I care about you and I don't want you to feel like you are alone. I want to be there by your side. Together we are stronger. Together we can win,' I said.

'You are already here with me,' he said. 'You have been by my side this whole time.'

'My flight is tonight,' I said. 'I hope that you are okay with this.'

Amar said nothing.

'Have you arrived?' I asked.

'Yes,' replied Amar. 'It's beautiful.'

'What can you see?' I asked.

'It's a beautiful lake. This place is calming. I love it here. I feel at peace,' he said. 'I found an article on this place. I'll read it. Grand Bassin is a crater lake situated in a secluded mountain area in the district of Savanne, deep in the heart of Mauritius. It is about 1800 feet above sea level. The first group of pilgrims who went to Ganga Talao were from the village of Triolet and it was led by Pandit Giri Gossayne from Terre Rouge in 1898. It is considered the most sacred Hindu place in Mauritius.'

'What are doing?' I asked.

'I'm just admiring the water,' he said. 'I think I'm going to pray.'

I listened quietly. Amar opened the yearn and scattered the remaining ashes into the river until it was empty. Amar took the stairway to the top of the mountain. At the top resided a giant statue of the monkey God Hanuman. He is the symbol of strength and energy. Amar walked up to it and prayed. I listened while Amar chanted a mantra. He told me once that he did not believe in God. He felt that a God cannot exist in a world like this, especially after everything that had happened to his family. Visiting this statue had given him faith.

He returned to his car.

'Are you okay?' I asked.

'Yes,' said Amar. 'I have decided something.'

'What is it?' I said.

'Don't try and stop me,' he said. 'I am going to the abandoned house. I'm going inside.'

'Please don't go,' I said. 'It's not safe.'

'I still have Maya's gun on me,' he said. 'I have nothing to fear. If I die tonight then I must accept it. I just want to know the truth. I want to lure the killer out. I don't even care if I kill him. I just want to stare into his cold lifeless eyes.'

Amar

Wednesday 25th February 2015

Afternoon

I drove back to the abandoned house. There was something that did not add up here. Maya was about to email me the photographs of my family moments before she was attacked. I needed to go back and see.

I phoned Doctor Addison and told her to stay on the phone in case anything happened. I drove up to the house. I still had the gun that Maya gave me and a golf club that I was going to use as a weapon.

There were lots of police cars patrolling Chemier Boulangerie and the surrounding area. I needed to wait until everything had died down.

I started to suspect Dev. Nobody else knew that I was here. How was the killer always one step ahead of me? What if Dev was behind everything? I didn't care at that point. I was inviting him to kill me to see if it was actually him. In a way, I wanted to die. I was ready to let go. All I cared about was finding out the truth. I wanted to look at the killer in his eyes. Nothing made sense. I wanted to understand why he was killing everybody.

I arrived near a wooden fence. It had gone dark. I felt frightened but I had to do it. There had to be a connection. There was little to go on. I was still shaken up by what happened to Maya.

Outside of the house, red tape had been strung from the

trees. The killer wanted me powerless and had succeeded. He could be hiding in the house, watching me, waiting. In the terrible silence and loneliness, I felt scared and wanted to pray again to God. In my mind, I could still hear her voice over the phone as she was being strangled.

I was no longer scared of this place. I replayed the terrifying scene in my mind over and over again. The killer was probably still in the area. I could be as patient as he was. I was hunting now. I watched for his face, his body language. The killer had grown too confident in himself. Blood had pumped loudly through my head. I was rapidly approaching the abandoned house.

I sprinted up closer to the house. I walked inside. I looked everywhere for the family photo album but I could not find it. Inside the ceiling was low, possibly under 8 feet. No windows in the room.

The door to a small closet was open halfway. I peered inside. What I remembered made me feel ill. Using my remaining strength, I concentrated hard to focus my eyes. I continued to stare. My eyes darted to the top of the antique dresser across the room. I was beginning to feel more clear headed. I didn't want to give myself an unnecessary headache. I had only one thought as I examined every single wardrobe.

I walked into my room and towards the closet where I hid all those years ago. On top of the bed lay the porcelain doll that I saw in the video. Someone must have moved it. I wish that my memory was better. The doll reminded me of something and looked as though it was watching me.

I grabbed it and threw it under the bed. I decided to keep looking. I walked into my parents room and looked everywhere. I wished that Maya had told me where she found the photo album. I kept on looking. I finally found a stack of photo albums upstairs in the study. This was where Maya was strangled.

It started to rain again. The rain pinged on top of the tin roof. The sound transported my mind back to when I was 5 years old and when Maya was strangled.

I heard loud police sirens. The police were here. If they caught me trespassing on the crime scene, I would be in a lot of trouble.

I grabbed the photo album and looked for a way to sneak out.

I looked for a window to climb out of.

I spotted a trail of blood.

I followed it and found Dev's lifeless body on the ground. He had been strangled to death and a blade had been driven into his stomach. He looked as though he had been dead for several hours. Someone left his body here to frame me. For a second, I thought what if I had done it? I panicked and scanned the room. The murderer was still here. What if I was the murderer? I was scared.

I ran out of the house.

'Stop,' shouted the police officers.

They all had their guns pointed at me.

'Don't move,' said one of the officers.

He tackled me to the ground and cuffed me.

'You are under arrest,' he said.

'It wasn't me,' I said.

I tried to explain what I could. I pleaded with them. I was telling the truth but even I didn't know for sure. I was brought to my knees. I could see the madness in my eyes as I looked at my reflection in the wing mirror of a police car. I was in shock and trembling with fear. It was finally over. I was the killer. I had to be.

I was charged for Dev's murder and possession of another officer's firearm. In a way, I was relieved. I did not want to see any more dead bodies. What if I had done it? I should have listened to my gut. I should have never come back here to look for the killer.

Doctor Addison

Wednesday 25th February 2015

Afternoon

Amar's phone disconnected while he was in the house. The killer could have gotten to him by now. I called Amar but I couldn't get through. How long should I wait until I contact the police. This was all my fault. I should have been there by his side. I could have stopped him. This plan was like a kamikaze attack. He had no chance. He was walking right into the killer's hand.

I got a call from a restricted number. I answered it.

'Hello this is Inspector Singh. We have Amar in our custody. What was he doing back at the crime scene?' he asked.

'He went to draw out the killer,' I said. 'I tried to stop him but he would not listen.'

'We caught him with a possession of a gun,' he said. 'It belonged to Inspector Maya.'

'She gave it to him,' I explained.

'We also found a male victim inside the abandoned house,' he said. 'He is dead. Lividity places the time of death at over 12 hours ago. We checked the whole house. There was nobody else there.'

'Somebody is setting him up,' I said. 'Who was the victim?'

'His name is Dev Shah,' he explained. 'He is a taxi driver. He drove Amar from the airport and around Montagne Blanche. What was he doing there?'

'Amar went there alone,' I said. 'I have no idea. Your guess is as good as mine but I remember Amar mentioning him.'

'You are his Doctor,' said Inspector Singh. 'Does Amar suffer from multiple personalities or any mental issues that may have contributed to this?'

'No,' I replied. 'Amar does not suffer from DID.'

'What about any dependencies on drugs or alcohol?' He asked.

'No,' I replied knowing fully well that I was lying. This was what Amar wanted. I was lying to the police to protect him.

'Amar is being framed,' I said. 'He was at his hotel when Detective Le Clezio was killed. Somebody else is setting him up. Amar does not have it him to kill. I am sure of it.'

'I have to go,' said Inspector Singh. 'I will be in touch.'

'What about Amar?' I asked. 'When can I speak to him?'

'He will call you when he is permitted,' replied Inspector Singh.

I hung up the phone. My flight was in a few hours. I knew that it was dangerous but I had no choice. I was tired of taking a back seat. I wanted to help. Amar's life was on the line. He had been through so much and he had nobody to support him apart from my voice over the telephone.

I arrived at Gatwick airport. I thought about turning back around and going home but I took a deep breath and got on the plane. My life had no excitement. This was my chance to do something good and help somebody. I know that I am risking my life but Amar could really use a friend.

Amar

Thursday 26th February 2015

Morning

The killer was always one step ahead. How did he know that I was at the crime scene? He was probably watching me this whole time. The police had me detained at the central prison in Beau Bassin. In a way, I was glad that I was here. I was safe here. I could see some buildings from the gap in my prison window. I did not want anyone else to die or get hurt. We were closer to the truth. The killer would slip up sooner or later. I could feel it.

I got charged with trespassing onto a crime scene, possession of an officer's firearm and they think that I killed Dev. Could I have killed him? It had to be somebody else. I don't remember strangling him and driving a blade into his stomach. The killer must be really light on his feet. I never heard or saw anyone else in the house.

I had a feeling that the porcelain doll was the key to all of this. I don't know what it was. I just had a hunch that it was alluding to something much greater. In my dreams, it was as though someone was warning me and trying to tell me something. I also could not understand how the doll moved from the closet to the top of the bed. Someone must have moved it.

I started thinking about Maya. I wondered how she was getting on. I imagined the existence of a certain place. Still incomplete. When I pictured this place it was misty and I could not see it clearly but there were indistinct outlines, vague yet I was sure that something absolutely vital laid for me. I imagined Maya waiting for me there. We were two pieces of the same face. I was one side and she was the other.

We were connected through our families. She was the only one that understood me. She felt exactly how I felt each day after the night of the 5th. Her family had perished before mine so she had carried this pain for even longer than me. I wanted to understand why we had suffered through all of this.

One of the guards knocked on my cell.

'I have a message from Inspector Singh,' he said.

'What is it?' I asked.

'Its Maya,' said the prison guard.

'How is she?' I asked.

'She's much better,' he replied. 'The Doctor just informed us that she will make a full recovery. I will keep you updated. Who could have done this?'

'Your guess is as good as mine,' I said.

Finally some good news. Last night, I dreamt that me and Maya lived together in South London. I didn't know much about her. The only thing connecting us was this case.

Why was Doctor Addison coming here? It made no sense. Why was she risking her life to help me? She mentioned that she was writing a book about all of this. She even asked for my permission. I said that it was fine. I wondered if we could ever be more than just Doctor and patient. I could not have done any of this without her. I don't think that I would have ever returned back here if it wasn't for her.

We were close. I could feel it. The killer was out there. He was watching us. I felt sorry for Dev. I should have never dragged him into this. Why was he killed? What was he doing at the crime scene? I felt sorry for him. What if I killed him? What if I have a split personality? Doctor Addison said that I did not exhibit any of the symptoms. What if it was dormant? I couldn't make sense of anything.

I was worried for Doctor Addison. I should have never asked her to come here. I never thought in a million years that she would do it. I hated that I planted the idea in her mind. I have to make sure that she doesn't get hurt. I told Inspector Singh to keep an eye on her and maybe assign some police officers to her. He said that he will see what he can do.

I wanted Doctor Addison to remain in London. I cannot understand how she can help. She was endangering her life.

Doctor Addison

Thursday 26th February 2015

Morning

I landed at the airport. I hailed a taxi. I decided to stay at the Grand hotel in Port Louis. Dev was murdered and Amar was the only other person at the homicide scene. I knew that Amar was innocent but all of the evidence was pointing to him. He was rotting in a jail cell. I called a solicitor for him. I wanted to help him.

I wondered if he was behind it all. What if Amar was the killer and he wanted me to say that he was clinically insane? Amar did not have it in him to kill. He had a good heart. Somebody was setting him up.

Amar was the only person at the crime scene. There was no evidence that anyone else was on the premises. Amar was my patient and I cared for him. I wanted to help him but I couldn't make any sense of anything. I just wanted the nightmares to stop. I wanted the little girl to leave me alone.

I arrived at the police station with Detective Shen. We spoke to Amar through the visitors glass and a telephone. I managed to get his side of the story. I told him not to worry and that everything would turn out alright.

Amar had a hunch.

He asked Detective Shen to retrieve the porcelain doll from the abandoned house. He wanted to know who made it.

Amar grew more fixated with the porcelain doll. Detective Shen thought that he was going insane. We both dreamt of a little girl holding onto a porcelain doll. There was no way to prove that anything was connected. Everything was speculative. We needed hard evidence.

'Kate, I want you to go back to London. It's not safe,' said Amar. 'You cannot stay here.'

'I hired a solicitor for you,' I said. 'We have to prove to the jury that there is somebody else at hand. The fact that you have a bulletproof alibi for Detective Le Clezio's murder and Maya's attack will cause doubt over whether it was actually you that killed Dev.'

'Promise me that you will not go anywhere near the abandoned house?' demanded Amar.

'I promise,' I said.

'I threw the porcelain doll under the bed in the last bedroom on the right,' said Amar.

'Amar we need to focus on your defence in court,' I said.

'No please. I need you to trust me,' said Amar. 'I have a feeling about this. We need to focus on the doll.'

I told him that me and Detective Shen would look into it.

Amar thanked me. He just wanted all of this to end. I tried to comfort him.

I told him not to give up.

I said goodbye and went outside for a smoke.

Detective Shen asked if I had a cigarette.

I gave him one.

'I can get someone to retrieve the porcelain doll from the house,' he said.

'Only if you think that it's safe,' I said.

I went back to the hotel.

Later that day, I got a message from Detective Shen. He said that he may have cracked this case. I called him.

'What have you found?' I asked.

'Brace yourself,' he said. 'I got somebody to go back to the crime scene to retrieve the porcelain doll. I have the doll on me now. I inspected the toy and it was what I thought.'

'What?' I asked.

'It's handmade,' he said.

'Are you sure?'

'Yes, I am sure,' he replied. 'And I know who made it.'

'Who?' I asked.

'A toymaker,' said Detective Shen.

'A toymaker?' I asked.

'Yes, a toymaker,' he said. 'He owns a shop in Montagne Blanche. He makes wooden ornaments and hand made toys.'

'I bet you that he is our guy,' said Detective Shen.

'We need to get a warrant to search his house. I bet that we find something that ties him to all of this,' I said.

I phoned Inspector Singh and explained the situation.

'Can we get a search warrant? I'm sure that we will find something,' I said.

'Are you sure?' asked Inspector Singh. 'It's a reach. All we have to go on is a porcelain doll. How does that tie him to all of this?'

'Amar's youngest sister Neha owned one of his handmade dolls,' I said. 'I know it probably sounds absurd but Amar has a feeling about it. His life is on the line here. We have to at least try. We both know that he didn't kill anyone. Someone is setting him up.'

'I will get a search warrant but I don't think that we will find anything.'

'Please Inspector,' I pleaded. 'Just promise me that you will try.'

'I will do my best,' he said.

I hung up the phone. We had our first lead. I wanted to tell the Inspector about my dream but I did not want to come off as a crazy person. Who was this little girl? Was she Neha? And who was this toymaker?

I wondered if Amar would remember the toymaker. His sister owned one of his handmade porcelain dolls. Maybe he was around when she bought it. I doubt that he would remember anything from that long ago.

I got news that Maya would make a full recovery. I was glad. I think that Amar is in love with her. I wished that I could be happy for him. I wished that Amar never slept with her. Those two are perfect for each other. Their trauma has brought them together. I guess we wont get a chance to go out for that drink like he promised me. Promises even vague ones like that linger in your mind. I wondered if he would ever return back to London. I don't think that he will. Maybe I can visit him in Mauritius. I like speaking to him. I can feel a proper connection. I haven't felt this way about someone in a very long time.

In the last couple of weeks, we have developed a strong connection. This predicament has brought us closer together. I love how he likes reading the same books as me. All my life, I have never met anyone like him. Psychiatrists are attracted to damaged people with mental baggage. Deep down we are drawn to these people because we think that we can fix them.

Am I drawn to Amar? Maybe I am. I wish that he never met Maya. Maybe they will break up and he will return back to London. My heart was racing and I was pacing up and down my hotel bedroom. I sat down at my desk and started writing.

Amar

Friday 27th February 2015

Morning

My days feel empty now. I am finally getting used to the solitude. At least I am safe here.

I wish that I was anywhere but here. I wish that I could speak to Doctor Addison. When all of this is done we will probably go our separate ways. I will miss speaking to her. I think that she is an extraordinary woman. I have never met anyone like her.

She was just my Doctor. She was just doing her job. Maybe I should tell her how I feel. Why spoil a good friendship and make things awkward.

I thought about Maya. I haven't slept with anybody else since my ex. I had forgotten all about my ex. I don't even miss her anymore. She was the past and this was the present. I need to look at what's in front of me.

I can't wait to see Maya. I want to spend every second with her. I want her to get better. I don't know if she will forgive me. I'm sure that she will understand. I had no idea that her family were murdered.

Back then, I honestly thought that she was trying to kill me. The door that lead into Maya's world had been shut behind me. I wanted to hear from her lips that her feelings were the same.

I am alone here with my thoughts. I don't have anyone to talk to. I am only granted visitors and phone calls on certain days. I bet that there will come a time when I will not get any visitors for weeks and even months. I will probably get used to the loneliness. It feels like I belong here. Maybe I never belonged out there.

I heard a thud from a police baton against my cell. It was the guard.

'You have visitors,' he said.

'Who is it?' I asked.

'It's Inspector Singh and 2 other people. They want to speak to you. They said that it was urgent,' explained the prison guard.

I wondered what couldn't wait until tomorrow.

I walked out of my cell and into an interrogation room. Police Inspector Singh, Detective Shen and Doctor Addison were waiting for me.

Doctor Addison ran up to me and hugged me. She asked me how I was doing.

'Fine,' I said.

'Sit down,' said Inspector Singh.

I took a seat.

Detective Shen opened his bag. He took out a porcelain doll.

'Is that Neha's doll?' I asked.

'Yes,' replied Inspector Singh.

The doll was very dirty. The Private Investigator had not cleaned it and he wore gloves.

'Can you remember how your sister got this toy?' asked Inspector Singh.

I closed my eyes and tried to remember.

'I'm sorry,' I said. 'It was a long time ago.'

'We have tracked down the person who made it. Its hand crafted from a shop in Montagne Blanche,' explained the Private Investigator.

'I do remember a shop,' I said. 'We went there a few days before Christmas. How is the toymaker connected to all of this?'

'I don't know but it's our only lead,' replied Inspector Singh. His word rustling like leaves. 'We are going to search his place of residence and his shop. Maybe we'll find something.'

'I hope so,' I said.

Doctor Addison hugged me and told me that everything was going to be alright. I put my arms around her. I did not want to let her go.

I thanked everyone and returned back to my cell.

Doctor Addison

Friday 27th February 2015

Afternoon

Inspector Singh demanded that I meet him at the lobby of the Grand hotel. I got in his car.

'What is it?' I asked.

'I have assigned 2 officers to you. Make sure that you stay with them at all times,' he said.

'What happened?' I asked.

'We found the murder weapon,' said Inspector Singh. 'We also found Dev's blood on the sole of the toymaker's work boots but he has fled. He knew that we were coming after him. We found a camera hidden inside the doll's eyes.'

I shuddered.

'Do you think that he will come after me?' I asked.

'Yes,' he said. 'That's why you will be under police protection until we catch him. There is a nationwide manhunt for him. His name is Peter Sarstedt. Here is a picture of the suspect.'

I glanced at the photograph.

'Does this mean that Amar can go free?' I asked.

'Yes,' he said.

'When?' I asked.

'Lets go now and we can also update him on everything,' suggested Inspector Singh.

I thanked him.

I got in his car.

'Amar is very lucky to have you,' said Inspector Singh. I smiled.

We arrived at the prison where Amar was detained. We finally got the break that we were looking for.

I was overjoyed. Words could not express how I felt. I guess my little story will have a happy ending.

I kept wondering how the toymaker was connected to all of this?

I wanted to write. My story had reached its climax. This was the part when everything would tie together.

I ran up to Amar and hugged him.

'How is Maya doing?' he asked.

'She is much better,' said the Inspector. 'I want this case closed once and for all.'

'I am just happy that Amar can finally find peace,' I said.

'It isn't over just yet,' said Amar. 'We still don't know why he did it.'

'Yes that's right,' I said.

'I don't think that we could have cracked this case without you two. You make a good team,' said Inspector Singh.

'We are happy to have helped,' I said.

We drove to the hospital to visit Maya. Amar walked up to her and hugged her.

'How are you?' he asked.

'I am fine,' said Maya.

'I'm sorry that we didn't trust you,' said Amar.

'You should have told us about your parents,' I said. 'We had no idea. I'm sorry.'

'Is that your girlfriend? I mean the Doctor?' asked Maya.

'Yes that's my psychiatrist,' replied Amar. 'She is not my girlfriend. Did you get a look at the suspect?'

'He was a tall man wearing all black and he had on a white mask covering his face,' said Maya. 'He was very strong and well built. Does any of this ring a bell?'

Inspector Singh showed Maya a picture of the suspect.

'We searched the suspect's place of residence but he had fled by the time we got there. He had a camera installed in the doll's eyes. He heard us talk. He was watching us this whole time.'

'Maya,' said Inspector Singh. 'I have assigned 2 police officers to remain with you at the hospital to keep you safe. Don't leave their sight for a second until we catch Peter Sarstedt.'

'Yes sir,' said Maya. 'When can I go back to work?'

'Not anytime soon,' he said. 'And I want the 2 of you to return back to the Grand hotel in Port Louis. My officers will escort you back.'

'Okay,' I said. 'Amar lets go.'

'Wait,' said Maya. 'Can I speak to Amar for a second in private?'

'Yes sure,' replied Amar.

We left Amar and Maya alone in the hospital room. I was waiting outside the door.

I peered through the glass window. I wanted to hear what they were talking about.

Amar leaned in and hugged her. Then he kissed her on the lips. I looked away.

He was still kissing her.

I wanted to look away.

I walked to the end of the corridor.

I should have never come here.

Amar walked out to meet us.

Two officers drove us back to the Grand hotel.

Me and Amar was sat in the back seat.

'Thank you for being here,' he said.

'What did Maya speak to you about?' I asked.

'It was nothing,' he said. 'I am really glad that I met her. For the first time in my life, I don't feel alone.'

Doctor Addison

Saturday 28th February 2015

Morning

Where am I? How did I get here. I slowly opened my eyes.
My hands were tied up to a chair. Amar was tied opposite
to me.

'Wake up,' I said. 'Amar wake up.'

I nudged him with my shoulder. He slowly opened his
eyes.

'Where are we?' asked Amar.

'I don't know,' I said. 'How did we get here?'

'I don't remember. Where are the police officers? I
remember how they were driving us back to our hotel,'
said Amar.

A tall man wearing a white mask entered the room.

'We know who you are,' said Amar. 'Peter Sarstedt. Why
are you hiding behind that mask?'

He didn't take it off. He came closer. He was studying us.
We were his victims, his prey.

'Let her go,' said Amar. 'She doesn't have anything to do
with this. Before you kill me. Just tell me why? Why did
you kill my family? Why did you kill Maya's family? Why
did you kill Detective Le Clezio? Why did you kill Dev?'

'She was a customer from my store,' explained Peter
Sarstedt.

'Who?' asked Amar.

'The little girl,' he said. 'I gave her one of my handmade dolls a long time ago on Christmas Eve. She and her mother were homeless. One evening, the little girl was in my store as I was closing up. She looked distraught. She was crying. I asked her what was wrong. She told me that her mother was killed. She got run over by a drunk. That drunk was your father Amar. Your father killed her and left her at the side of the road to die. She also told me all about Maya's father. The horrible policeman who refused to help her. She had been alone and hungry. She really missed her mother. I told her that I would take care of her. I told her to stay put and I went to get her a cup of hot chocolate. I came back and she was gone. I ran out of the shop and looked everywhere for her. I couldn't find her anywhere. I wanted to help her. She had nobody. I thought that she would return back to my shop. I waited for days but she never came back. I went to the local police station. I showed them a picture of the little girl. The policeman said that the girl had died a few days ago. She had drowned herself at the Sans Souci water reservoir. I blamed myself. I should have helped her. I should have done more. I decided to go to the police. I explained what the little girl had told me. That's when I spoke to Maya's father. He refused to help me. I had no evidence and he told me that I was just wasting his time. He told me to forget about all of this. I walked out of the police station enraged. I thought that was the end of it all but I was wrong. The little girl has haunted my dreams ever since that night. She wanted me to help her get justice. That's when I snapped. That's when I took action. I killed everyone and she promised me that she would stop appearing in my dreams. She told me that you would be coming. She wanted you and Maya to feel exactly how she felt. She wanted you powerless. I just want her to leave me alone. I have tried everything. I have killed everyone that she had asked me to kill but she still won't leave me in peace. I am just glad that it is finally over.'

'How is it over?' asked Amar.

'First, I am going to blow your brains away with this gun. Then I will do the same to me,' explained Peter Sarstedt.

Amar

Saturday 28th February 2015

Morning

I heard police sirens.

How do they know that we are here?' asked Peter Sarstedt. 'You two. One of you must have.'

Peter looked angry.

Suddenly shots rang out. Peter untied Doctor Addison and dragged her away with a gun pointed at her head.

'Let her go,' I said. 'Take me instead.'

Peter Sarstedt fled with Doctor Addison. I pleaded with him and asked him to let the Doctor go.

Maya burst on the scene with a team of police officers. She untied me.

'We have to find them,' I said. 'He has Doctor Addison with him.'

We were in an abandoned multi storey car park. The police officers chased after him. They had him cornered. Maya and the other police officers were all pointing their guns at him.

'You are surrounded. Let her go,' demanded Maya.

'Put your guns down now or I am going to jump and I am going to take her with me,' said Peter Sarstedt. 'Or how about I just paint the floor with her brains. Guns on the ground now.'

Everyone lowered their guns and placed them on the ground.

Peter Sarstedt pushed Doctor Addison forward.

'I'm sorry,' said Peter Sarstedt, 'She made me do it. It's not my fault. It's the little girl's fault. It's not my fault.'

Peter Sarstedt leaped over the edge of the building. His body floated down like a tiny droplet. We ran up to the edge.

A loud thud rang out. His body splattered all over the ground. He was dead.

It was finally over. I finally got the answer that I was looking for. I ran up and hugged Doctor Addison.

'Thank you,' she said. 'Thank God it's over.'

Doctor Addison

Sunday 1st March 2015

Evening

I decided to leave without saying goodbye to Amar. I wanted to tell him how I felt but I didn't want him to decide between me and Maya. I was afraid that he would choose her. He clearly liked her. He was in love with her and she loved him.

Maybe it won't work out between them and he will return to London.

'Kate,' somebody shouted my name.

I turned around. It was Amar.

'What are you doing here?' I asked.

Amar was out of breath and panting.

'Why didn't you say goodbye?' he said.

'I have to get back to work,' I said.

'I didn't get a chance to say thank you,' said Amar.

'You have already thanked me,' I replied.

'What's the rush?' asked Amar. 'I was going to take you to see that underwater waterfall. I already booked the helicopter.'

'You should have said something,' I said. 'I just thought that you would be busy because of Maya. I know that you like her.'

'It's just,' he took a breath. 'I feel like I owe you for helping me and I promised to take you out for a drink. Remember?'

'I remember,' I said. 'If you ever come back to London. Call me and we will arrange it. You are still my patient Amar. I want you to call me anytime that you are confused or if you just want to talk. My door will always be open to you. This is not goodbye.'

Amar opened his mouth like he was going to say something but the words had evaporated off his tongue.

Amar leaned in and hugged me. His eyes started tearing.

'I could not have done this without you,' he said.

'Last call for flight 245 to London Gatwick. Gate shuts in 10 minutes,' said the announcement.

'Amar I have to go,' I said.

'Please don't go,' he said. 'Stay here with me. I don't want to say goodbye.'

'This is not goodbye,' I said. 'You can call me anytime. I will be in London waiting for you.'

'Okay,' he said.

Amar leaned in and hugged me.

'I love you,' I whispered.

'What did you say?' asked Amar.

'I said that I have to go,' I replied. 'I am going to miss my flight.'

I grabbed my suitcase and walked to my gate. I wanted to turn around and look but I didn't. My eyes started to tear up. I just wish that I could hold him. I wished that he just grabbed me and kissed me. Why didn't he try to kiss me? Why did I say I love him? I don't think that he heard it. I have to get out of here. I just want to run away.

Amar

Sunday 1st March 2015

Evening

What just happened? I wanted to kiss her but something stopped me. I should have just gone for it. I thought I heard her say that she loves me but I don't think that she said that. She said that she had to go. My mind was playing tricks on me again.

I felt so torn. I did not understand what was happening. I did not know what to do.

I got a message. It was from Maya. She asked me what I was doing? She wanted to meet up with me at the Grand hotel in an hours time.

I told her that I was on my way.

I got in my car and drove. The road was long and winding.

I slowed my car down and parked on the side of the road.

I took out my phone and looked at flights to Gatwick. There was another flight in 4 hours. I had an open return ticket. I wanted to do the right thing but I didn't know what that was. I was confused.

I wish that I had a sign. Should I tell the Doctor how I feel or should I tell Maya how I feel? I was in love with both of them. I wished that I didn't have to make this decision. I wished that I leaned in and kissed Doctor

Addison. I wished that she kissed me back. I wished that I told her how I felt. I wished that I told her that I love her.

I can't forget about Maya. She saved my life. She risked everything to help me. Every kiss from her lips felt like my soul was on fire. What should I do? I wish that I didn't have to make this decision.

I took a deep breath and closed my eyes. I decided to follow my heart.

The End

PLEASE SUBSCRIBE TO THE PUBLISHER'S
MAILING LIST BY VISITING

www.boathousepublishing.com

for blog content and information on future releases.

ALSO AVAILABLE

Christmas Eve At Kentwood Park

By Hans Seesarun

Kevin and his mother are hiking through Kentwood Park on Christmas eve. They soon realise that they are lost and his mother slips and is knocked unconscious. Kevin is all alone and his mother is slowly dying. Determined to save her, he bravely sets out into dangerous and forbidden territory all alone in the dark after the park is closed.